A Breakthrough Book
No. 54

Testimony

Stories by
Jean R. Matthew

University of Missouri Press
Columbia, 1987

Library of Congress Cataloging-in-Publication Data

Matthew, Jean R.
Testimony: stories.

✓ (A Breakthrough book; no. 54)
Contents: Sweet Letty – The letters of Mrs. J. L.
Hartle – The life and death of Martha – [etc.]
I. Title. II. Series.
PS3563.A8395T4   1987   813'.54   86-16126
ISBN 0-8262-0623-9 (alk. paper)

This book was brought to publication with the assistance
of a grant from the National Endowment for the Arts.

The author would like to thank the following journals for
permission to reprint stories that first appeared in their
pages: *Crescent Review* for "Family Visit" (Vol. 4, No. 1)
and "The Letters of Mrs. J. L. Hartle" (Vol. 3, No. 1);
Southern Humanities Review for "Sweet Letty" (Vol. XIX,
No. 4, Fall 1985); and *Wind Magazine* for "The Life
and Death of Martha" (Vol. 16, No. 57, 1986).

For Charlotte Gafford,
John, and Malcolm,
Matt, and Johnathan

Contents

Sweet Letty

Sweet Letty danced in front of the fat mirror. She stepped up close and backed off, then held her hem in a curtsy and kicked up the powdery dust with her bare feet. Her long white hair was yellowed at the ends, like tobacco-stained fingers. Her small face was flat and her tongue stuck out, just barely. In the mirror her body looked like a pale balloon. May stood next to her with her arms at her sides and studied the dance. In the fat mirror the sisters were raw-boned women. May's hair was still brown, and she was small and finely wrinkled.

Two small boys in short pants watched a fat man play the calliope. The man held a pipe in his front teeth and wore tiny wire-rimmed spectacles. One of the boys spit in a stream through his front teeth.

The mirror was new to Sweet Letty every spring. She behaved as if she had never seen it before, as if it were the most curious thing in the show. The mirror was flaked and covered with small black dots.

Behind them Mac the barker yelled. He was as spindly as a walking stick. There was a pie-shaped piece out of the brim of his top hat, and his coat was worn to a beetle green in places. He pointed and stuck out his chin at passersby.

"This way. This way for the strange happenings of Mother Nature. See them here. Not for ladies and children. Strong men only. Step this way. See Miss Arie, the fattest woman in ten counties. See all of her. See Tina, the woman with flippers. See lovely Miss May dance the dance of the east with the deadly six-foot snake."

*   *   *

Every spring they came together in front of the county

courthouse: the animal tender, Mac the barker, Sam the backup man, Miss Arie, Tina, and May and her dim-witted sister. They met old Bart, and they started off, always on a Sunday morning. They followed the same circuit, had followed it for close to thirty years. In that time there had been few changes. May and Sweet Letty had joined after their mama had run off with a fancy man who wore vanilla for scent. Bart was distant kin on their daddy's side, and May could not take care of Sweet Letty alone. There had been twin fan dancers, Fran and Dolly, but they had left to work in a defense plant and had married soldiers. Georgina, the fat lady, had died, and Miss Arie had filled her place.

They drove slowly, blocking narrow dirt roads and taking full days to go less than a hundred miles. Bart Whitefeather was never in a hurry; Sam said he went by Indian time, not white man's.

They were in the third week of another season, dogwood and violet days. May and Sweet Letty walked through the poor crowd, through vapors of sour sweat and Lily-of-the-Valley toilet water, boiled peanuts and cotton candy. A little girl with a baby on her hip stood charmed in front of Mac. The baby rested its big head on her shoulder and sucked a dirty fist. Three young men smoked and watched the Ferris wheel turn with no one on it. One of them flicked his cigarette into the path. May guided Sweet Letty around the ember.

They stopped in front of the animal pens. The monkey jumped at them, then sat back on his haunches and worried a tuft of fur on his arm. He stared at them, looking like an old black man, wrinkled and the color of pencil lead. In the next pen the bear sat with his legs out stiff, holding onto his feet. He yawned and showed pink and brown gums and the wide, gray ridges of the roof of his mouth. May picked up peanuts from the ground and gave them, one by one, to Sweet Letty who threw them at the bear. He felt along the floor of his cage after them. His eyes were clouded with cataracts. The monkey reached his skinny arm through the slats, and Sweet Letty put a peanut in his paw. Then she put a peanut shell in her own mouth and choked. May reached down her throat

2

and pounded her back until the shell came out. Sweet Letty cried with no sound and covered her face with her hands. She would not move until May pulled her along by the elbow.

* * *

At the cotton candy stand they stopped, and May got her a cone. "Behave now," she told Sweet Letty.

The trucks and trailers were lined up in a caravan beyond the midway on the edge of a weed-filled field. The pickups had homes on their backs, cabins with windows and doors, the sides painted like turtles, with advertisements for the show. May and Sweet Letty lived with Bart on the back of a dull black 1938 Ford. Painted on both sides of the cabin in chipped red and yellow letters was "Whitefeather Shows. Attractions. Freaks. Conjuration. Rides. Fun." The door at the back of the cabin hung open.

Inside Bart fried thick slices of bologna on a small gas ring. He killed flies with a rusty fly swatter in one hand and pushed the bologna around in the skillet with a fork in the other. His hair in gray-streaked braids and around his wrists were twisted strings of red wool and cotton. He wore denim overalls and a red fringed shawl across his shoulders.

On both sides of the cabin were planks covered with cracked green oilcloth and above the planks were bunks. The ceiling was hung with bunches of dried galax, twinleaf, snakeroot, and cranesbill, all covered with cobwebs and turning like spiders in the heat of Bart's cooking.

May reached for a rag and wiped the pink, sticky mess from Sweet Letty's mouth and chin. She took the empty cone and tossed it out the door. Sweet Letty put her arms around May's neck and kissed her full on the mouth. She hung on May and pulled her off balance.

"I don't want sticky kisses now. Go outside if you're going to be a bother." May freed herself and steered Sweet Letty down the steps.

Bart handed May a plate with two curled slices of crisp bologna and a piece of store bread spread with catsup. "You know, that candy don't do her no good. Makes me sick, that stuff." He ate his meat from the end of a fork and pointed at May with it as he spoke. "Your snake is doing poorly."

"If it ain't her, it's that snake for me to worry on. I try to get her to eat. You know that. I believe she only lives for two things, that mirror and a whole spring and summer of cotton candy." May stood in the doorway, one hand on her flat hip.

Sweet Letty sat at the bottom of the steps. She pulled the soft dust between her legs and made piles with both hands. There were circles on either side of her, traced in the dirt and with bits of paper and cigarette butts in each. She patted the dirt pile flat and began over, pulling the dust back into a mound.

Bart speared another slice of meat from the pan. "She like to blow us all up this morning. She turned the gas on when you was out." He threw his bread crusts out the door. Sweet Letty stood them on edge in front of her. "She's got less sense every day."

It wasn't that she had less sense. Bart forgot about how bad off Sweet Letty was, the same way Sweet Letty forgot about the mirror. May brought Sweet Letty back inside and sat her at the window.

Four boys walked across the field. They stopped and looked down at the ground, then moved along.

"Look out there," May said. "See them boys? They appear to be searching for something. What do you think? Maybe they're looking for your good sense that got lost. Or maybe bird nests."

Sweet Letty reached out for May's neck. May pushed her around to the window. Sweet Letty pressed her face against the glass and licked the pane.

"That's right. Kiss the window. Be nice."

May padlocked the door behind her and turned the gas off at the tank. She put the key inside the paper cone and pushed it under the steps, then walked around to the window. Sweet Letty had her face pressed against the glass. She looked like a fish. May waved to her.

Bart was standing with his hands folded under his chin, looking up. Clouds moved in front of the sun. May watched them take shapes, like the fantastic pickled shapes in jars, ragged human likenesses. The clouds formed and re-formed until they stretched across the sky like blurred words.

"I don't want to hear no more about that snake being sick," May said. "He's like any old man in the spring, stiff and dull until the weather turns for good."

She followed Bart along the path past the backsides of tents and booths. There was the smell of grease and hot motors and the whine of an unmuffled motorcycle. The small Ferris wheel screeched and stopped overhead. The baskets swayed, and the riders screamed their thrill. The wind blew up dust and pieces of straw around May's ankles, picked up paper cones and peanut bags and cellophane wrappers. Her hair blew into her mouth. She went between the tents and out on the midway to tell Mac she was getting ready. Along the rails of the gangway to her tent were more signs: "Fortunes 25 cents. Pickled Human Horrors 10 cents. Real Live Snake Dance 50 cents."

King lay in the far corner of his pen. He looked as if the air had been let out of him. May knelt and reached in to him and ran her hand down his patterned back. The yellow of him had gone dull, and his eyes were milky. She picked his head up and held it in her hand.

"Come on, King. Liven up. It's spring already."

She stood and pulled her yellow dress over her head. Underneath, her skin was like vellum, and she wore only a pair of black rayon panties with rows of tarnished sequins hanging from threads. She wet two fingers and retied the loose knots. Then she smoothed her hair back and wound the phonograph. She saw the crowd through the tent flap.

The front row was full. She smelled whiskey, manure, the sharp smell of green aftershave. The rows in back filled, and she watched as farmers and millhands, two young soldiers and several young boys, sidled in and took places. She saw familiar faces, men who came every year and stood with their mouths hanging open, and each year they were more grizzled and aged. She grew old with them.

She dropped the needle on the record. The high-pitched flutes and distant drumrolls made the men cheer and shout.

They called her name.

She draped King around her neck and started the record over. He felt like a limp, soft rope, but heavy. His head and tail reached to the top of her panties and his body covered her small breasts. She parted the curtain and stepped on the stage, a smile on her face.

It was the same dance every time. She began with a strut across the stage, then leaned forward toward the men in the front row. She felt their breath and pulled back, arching her body. She kept time with her right foot, counting silently. The snake was still. She slid him down into her panties, first his head and then his tail. He was like a tailor's measure. She coiled him across her outstretched arms, and the men whistled when her breasts were bared. She moved her torso from side to side and rolled her hips as she brought the snake's head and tail together across her breasts. She danced in a circle, and, when she turned back to the crowd, the snake's head bulged in her crotch. With a finger, she pulled the elastic of her panties out and stood, the snake covering her. The crowd yelled louder as she wiggled backward, hands on her hips. The snake hung from her neck into her crotch. She stepped back and lifted him onto her shoulders. He stiffened and stuck his tongue out. Taking small steps, she moved to the rear of the stage and held the snake taut over her head. Then she stepped behind the curtain and took the needle off the record.

The men were crude and coarse, and they bellowed for her. She closed her eyes and concentrated on pictures she had seen in magazines. She thought of the little dog so small it fit into a teacup and a flea circus with invisible fleas jumping through hoops and pulling carts behind them. She stuck her fingers in her ears, and the noise became the sound of a wasp's nest, a sharp drone.

When she opened her eyes and took her fingers out of her ears, Sam was hollering through a megaphone, "Go on now, or I'll get the law. You got what you paid for, and that's all there is!"

May took King from her neck and put him in his pen. Then she wiped the sweat from her body with her dress. She pulled it on and sat beside King, her hand on his head. He was a good-natured snake. He kept the show clean of mice and helped them all make a living.

After her last show, May went to Bart's tent and sat where she could see and hear. She learned some of his secrets, his wise ways. She hunkered down and peeked through a hole.

Bart was conjuring. He sat with his back stiff, smoke from a cedar stick filling the air. Across from him sat a young woman with buck teeth. She wore a large picture hat with paper hydrangeas on top. Bart raised his arms. They came out from his sides like chicken wings. When he held his hands out, they trembled with the palsy. He chanted through his nose. On the table in front of him were several bunches of white feathers, a pile of small bones, a candle, and a basket filled with dried herbs and roots. He took a pinch of the herbs and dropped it on the candle flame. The smell was like peppermint and cold metal. He spit on his fingers and pinched the glow off the cedar stick.

"Tie a knot in the corners of your bedsheet." He held his hands steady in front of him. The woman took coins from her cloth purse and pushed them across the card table. She got up and backed out of the tent.

A spent woman in a faded housedress pushed a little boy in front of her. His scalp was patchy with ringworm. "Can you cure him?" she asked. "He's got the pinkeye."

* * *

The sky was black, and the wind blew harder. It pulled at the ragged bottoms of the tents, blew the wooden signs down, whipped more trash and dirt around. The cotton candy man boarded up his stand and shouted at May as she walked by, but the wind carried his words away. A couple shoved past May, the girl's long hair blowing against the sides of her face as she leaned into the wind. May walked with her head down to keep the sand and grit from her eyes. She had goosebumps on her bare arms.

Miss Arie sat on a wide platform in front of her trailer, a kerosene lamp beside her. She had peroxide ringlets and her hands couldn't quite meet across her belly. Tears ran down her face. Rain caused her to study on the Great Flood and the tears of her Lord.

May stopped and patted Miss Arie's wide knee. The fat woman smelled like old buttermilk. She nodded at May and wiped her face on her sleeve.

Beyond Miss Arie's, Sam sat in the cab of his truck. He was a sorry man, scarred from the fistfights he always won. "What the hell's with that snake?" He talked around the wad in his mouth.

"He's sick and old, that's what." May shouted through her hands to make him hear her.

"Get old Bart to stuff him with magic herbs. Just wring his neck and stuff him!" He rolled his window up.

Inside the cabin Sweet Letty sat in a pile of bedclothes and played with her rag doll. May lit a lamp, then took her by the shoulder and looked into her eyes.

"Listen up. Your dolly gots to eat. If you don't feed her, she'll take sick. Lose her wits like you. Or go belly up, like that snake." She handed Sweet Letty a slice of cold bologna. "Now you show Dolly you eat good. Show her it tastes nice."

Sweet Letty smelled the bologna, then took a small bite. She laid the meat over Dolly's face and spit at May.

May took her by the nose and chin and clamped Sweet Letty's mouth shut. Sweet Letty looked up and sputtered into her sister's hand.

May backed off and wiped her hand on her dress. She threw a piece of bread on the floor in front of Sweet Letty.

"You'll always eat bread, won't you? Bread and candy. That's all that's fit for a girl with no wits. I'd like to put a slap on you. We know that won't make no difference. You'll scream and spit whenever you've a mind to."

Sweet Letty waved her bread at May and smiled. Her teeth were tiny and black. She broke off bits of bread and rolled them between her fingers into balls and put the balls on Dolly's body. When she had finished and every bit of bread was balanced on the doll, she ate the balls one by one. While she sucked and chewed, May brushed her hair.

"Well, I know you don't mean it. You got a pure conscience. You don't know what you're doing. I keep reminding myself. Why, you don't even know where you are. Well, you're here in this cold place, waiting for old Bart."

When Bart came in, he brought the rain with him. It hit the window and splashed in big drops against the glass. The wind blew the door back, out of his hand. The cabin shuddered with the gusts.

He lit the overhead gaslight and put a pot of water on. He nodded at Sweet Letty and wrapped his shawl tight around his stooped shoulders.

"It's cold in here for her," he said.

May brought the pile of bedcovers around Sweet Letty like a cape. She took a man's gray wool sweater from under her bedroll and put it on.

Bart stirred coffee grounds into the boiling water. When the pot came to boil a second time, he flicked drops of cold water in and turned the gas off. He poured their coffee.

"There's going to come a day," he started.

"When I don't come down from the mountains," May finished for him. "And what will you do then? Hang a big wooden feather in front of your shack? Paint directions on rocks and barn roofs, Bart Whitefeather, this way?"

In the winter Bart went to the mountains, and May and Sweet Letty moved into Coosa, to Aunt Vee's Home for Boarders. They took walks through town and listened to the parlor radio every night, waiting for spring.

Bart handed May a cup of coffee and Sweet Letty a half-full glass of coffee and sugar. "Well, some day I will give it up, just won't come down in the spring." He held his mug in both hands and inhaled the steam.

May pulled on a pair of socks. "Some day. I hope by then I'll be ready to go on relief. It won't take long to go through the pitiful sum I've set by."

"When it comes," he said, "it'll be like any other day, won't be no big surprise. Happens, and that's that."

May shivered. "A rabbit's walking over my grave. At least I know I'll be buried in the woods."

They sat in the white glare of the gas lamp and drank their coffee. When they had done, Bart held his mug over his head and swirled it around three times. He turned it upside down on a saucer and read the grounds. They pointed to the east, the direction the show was going. There was a woman in them, and a dog with three legs. The wind died down, and the rain on the roof sounded like fat popping in a pan. Bart put on his bifocals, and he and May read from a water-stained book of herbs and remedies. He smiled and nodded at the places where he agreed, and he had her mark again the places where he disagreed. Sweet Letty played peekaboo with Dolly until she fell asleep on the floor. Long after May was in bed, Bart sat cross-legged on the floor, and the murmur of his prayers put her to sleep.

In the morning the sky had cleared, and dew lined the spiderwebs stretched across yarrow stalks in the field. Bart made corn cakes, and May dipped pieces in sorghum for Sweet Letty. After breakfast, he went to mend tents, and May and Sweet Letty went for their walk.

They took the path that led around the show, to the fat mirror. They walked past mud puddles, and Sweet Letty touched the oil rainbows with her toes. The rain had brought a thick smell of roses and honeysuckle and the warm decay of spring. Sweet Letty walked splayfooted through each puddle. May watched her clumsy, rolling walk and thought about how she looked like a child in the mud and a crooked old woman as she walked.

They stood in front of the mirror, and Sweet Letty danced. She watched herself with more attention, moving sideways slowly and seeing the reflection slide off the surface. She had never looked for herself behind the mirror, the way small children always did, and May knew it was not because she knew better. She marched in place and splashed orange mud against the mirror and up her legs. She reached out and placed her palm on her reflection.

The bear was curled up in a corner, and Sweet Letty threw a pebble at him, but he didn't move. The monkey ran back and forth, his tail kinked. He smelled like wet wool, and, when he sat down, he picked at a sore on his neck. Sam threw dirty straw in through the slats. He pulled a cigar from his pocket and bit the end off, spitting it into the monkey's cage. "I bet I could teach that monkey to chew and spit," he said. He gave the cigar ring to Sweet Letty. She put it on her thumb, then looked up at him and patted his hard belly.

King lay stretched out. He moved toward May and Sweet Letty. May draped him around her neck, and they went out into the sun. She set him down beside a puddle and splashed the warm water over him. Sweet Letty pulled at him, and, when she would not stop, May took him back inside. He moved across the straw with a dry rustle.

Sweet Letty walked along the empty midway, behind the tents to the field. May kept on her heels. The sun was hot, and the water in the puddles was tepid. Mud oozed between her toes. Sweet Letty headed toward two figures on the other side of the field.

It was a boy and his goat. The goat was small and brown and so was the boy. He was the color of root beer, and his hair was clipped so short his scalp showed. He held the goat by a short, frayed hemp rope. The goat tugged at it and chewed on tufts of grass. Sweet Letty stopped in front of them. She patted the goat on the head.

"Hello, ma'am. This here's my goat, my very own. To raise up."

"Well, it's very pretty," May told him.

Sweet Letty had bent over the goat. She grabbed it and kissed its muzzle. The boy jerked at the rope. Sweet Letty pulled, and she and the goat fell, the goat in her lap. She sat in the mud and held the goat's neck awry. The boy looked at her and at the goat, then up at May.

"Ma'am, I don't mean nothing, but it's my goat. She be hurting it!" He turned to Sweet Letty. "Please, ma'am, let it go!" He backed away, tried to pull the goat free, but Sweet Letty held fast.

They stopped, Sweet Letty and the boy and the goat, their eyes wide. The goat made a small choking sound in its throat. May saw that in the eyes of the goat and the eyes of Sweet Letty there was the same mean animal wisdom. She tugged at Sweet Letty's arms, trying to loosen the grip on the goat's neck.

"She don't mean harm. She don't know her own strength."

The goat was free, and the boy backed away, but it would not budge. He dropped the tether and took the goat by its legs and dragged it to him. Then he turned, and taking the rope in both hands he ran from them, the goat behind and trying to catch up. They ran to the edge of the field and out to the road beyond.

May watched them until they were out of sight, until they had disappeared in the shadow of the live oaks along the road. She felt out of sorts and annoyed, as if she had been waked in the night and did not know why. She was tired. She helped Sweet Letty to her feet and started back off across the field. Sweet Letty took off after the boy and the goat, pointing and making grunts at May.

"I'm in no mind to play," May told her. "You come on now, or you can go off and get yourself lost. You just keep walking that way."

May felt stiff and slow as she moved toward the caravan. It was blurred in the distance, like the mountains in their mist. Bart was a small, red dot at the truck. She thought she saw him wave, and she waved back. Behind her, Sweet Letty made the low animal sound she made when she was scared. May turned to her and saw that she stood halfway between Bart and Sweet Letty. Sweet Letty had her arms outstretched and she moaned.

"All right, I'm standing here waiting for you!" The mud had dried on her feet, and the air felt the same temperature as her body. The only thing that was sharp and clear was the sound of the calliope.

The Letters of
Mrs. J. L. Hartle

Dear Violet,   November 1, 1947

This is your sister, writing to you from her new house in town.
We are finally out of the country, and we have all the things
in life. I know you have got hot water from the tap too, but
I don't believe Mama will ever get it. I got it here. We have
us a brand-new house that is one of the ones that is being
built for the GIs coming back, which my Joe is and which your
George will be when he gets out. I hope you can get you a
new house, too. Where we are is called Friendly Acres, and
we will just see about that. Joe has got him a good job, and
that is good. Both my kids is about to go on to high school.
They do love it here. There is plenty for them to do. Susie
is going to be a regular Bowling Queen. And that Buddy is
always fixing some old car. When you have a new house, you
don't have to clean near so much.

Your loving sister, Rose Hartle.

Dear Violet,   May 16, 1948

Well, this is your sister again. I guess I take as long to write
back as you do, but then we always did. Things is going along
good. We are going to put in a little garden out back. That
is if we can keep the neighbor's kids and dogs out. I am not
going to put up canned goods, like Mama does, because Joe
is making good money, and I can buy easier at the big store.
The supermarket is better than the commissaries and the PX
for what they have. I never seen so much stuff in cans and

boxes! Living here is living in a real neighborhood. Do you have TV sets on that base? When George gets out, maybe you will move close to us. This place is filling up, but they keep building more houses every week.

Your loving sister, Rose Hartle.

Dear Violet,   December 29, 1948

You are not going to believe this, but we got us a TV, one of them big 12-inch ones in a blond cabinet, and a washing machine, not a wringer. It does the whole wash by itself. I hope you don't think I am throwing nothing in your face, but I know you are happy for me as you are my dear, only sister. When you and George come see us, bring your laundry, and we will do it. We have new people living next door. There was some with a big dog, which is gone. Thank God. Now there is a mixed couple. She is from overseas. He picked her up over there. She don't know our ways and is not fitting in. It is giving me some nerves. She hollers at the kids, mostly mine, which you know are good, and she don't even want them walking in front of that house!! I tell you, Violet, it is always something. They never had one decoration for Xmas on that house. I hope you had a good one.

Love from your sister, Rose. And her family, of course.

Dear Violet,   March 4, 1949

Well, I am sure Mama is getting to you, too, with her miseries with Pa. Now she has got that telephone out there, and don't she ring mine off the hook. Be glad you are not closer because it is a big mess. I have colored my hair with a new rinse, and it works better than any other I have used. Here is the end of the box if you want to give it a try. They have your color in it, too. We have been having to paint the rooms in the house as the paint has fell off in big flakes. Joe is working a lot extra to make more and keep that job. This life is sure different from the life in the country. Your niece and nephew are sure growing up. Susie is after the boys and sets her hair all the time. Buddy, he is fed up with schooling, but Joe won't let him give it up just yet. I am warning that Susie off the boys, but nobody could tell us when we were coming along. Of course, we didn't have near so much trouble to get into, did we? Here is this year's school pictures. Do not bend. Are you and George ever going to get here for a visit?

Love, your sister, Rose Hartle.

Dear Mama,   May 21, 1949

You know I am sorry for you that you are having trouble with Pa again, but them collect calls is running up the bill, and Joe don't like it. You know I can't say much as I never got on with Pa, and it's costing me something to listen to you. Since there really ain't nothing I can do to help you out, you had best stop making them calls, please. Or I will be having my own troubles right here, if you know what I mean. Joe has put his foot down. You could come and stay with us awhile, if that would help. You know you are welcome. Anytime.

Your daughter, Rose Hartle. Love to you, Mama.

Dear Violet,   July 8, 1949

I was glad to hear the news that George is getting discharged. Buddy is wanting to go in, like his father did and his favorite Uncle George. I just hope he don't go overseas and bring some foreign woman home. But his father didn't, ha ha, so I don't worry too much. We have been thinking about coming out home for a visit now that you will be there and since it don't look like none of you all are getting out this way, which is closer than you think, really. My Joe is working too hard, and he never took a vacation. And you know how *his* family is, I will not go see them. His sister run off with some sailor and left them kids with his mother to raise. So I was thinking to come and see you and George and the folks if that is OK. How is Mama? She don't write, and I think she is mad over them phone calls I put the stop to.

Your loving sister, Rose Hartle.

Dear Mama,   August 1, 1949

How is your garden? I guess you are pleased to have Violet and George with you. Of course, I didn't know what George's sister had done when I wrote to Violet. I didn't mean nothing, and I hope she knows it. Where is George going to get work out there? I hope they are going to help you out if they are going to live in your house. Which is something I never asked of you, and knock on wood, I surely hope I never have to. We are doing fine in town. I wish you would come and see my house, Mama. It still looks new. We got us a new used car, it is a Pontiac sedan. Joe give up on that old truck. But since you won't see us, we will come out home. See you soon.

Love, Rose.

Dear Violet,   December 1, 1949

I am writing you about Mama. She was so mean to me, as you know. And I am hurt. How was I to know she only wanted to see her precious grandson, Buddy? I never told her about all the trouble he has got into, and why does she think he went into the service in such a hurry? She never told me I had to bring him to get treated decent. And I wish you could talk to her about my Susie, too. Things is different now, and girls wear makeup when they want to. It don't mean that my Susie is not a nice girl. I don't mean for you to get in the middle or nothing, but I do not want me and my family on her bad side neither. The whole Thanksgiving was ruined by her meanness. She is getting old, and the old man is going to kill her with his drinking and his mean fits. I am sorry for you that George is not doing so good. He never did like it in the country. You could move here, there is always places coming empty. I hope you will talk to Mama about me.

Your loving sister, Rose.

Dear Buddy,   January 28, 1950

I am glad you lived through basic training. The other men in the family did, so you can, too. I know it must be hard with all kinds of people and coloreds, too. Thank God we don't have none· of that here. Yet! I don't know what you can do about your troubles getting along with them. You wanted to go into the service, you had to, and now you can just lie in it. You had better write a note to your grandmother. She was real put out that you was gone before we went there Thanksgiving. And you didn't go out there and see her before you left. She is getting along in years. We have had a little trouble, your dad and me, and had to give back our living room set, the one we got just before you left. Back to the finance company. Your father don't bring home his paycheck, and the bills is getting left. He is worse than he was when you left. I wish you'd never hit him, even if he was drunk. He is your father, and he will always be.

Your loving mother, Mrs. J. L. Hartle.

Dear Mama,   May 2, 1950

I am sure glad you got over that mean spell. We can't come out this spring because Joe is laid up for awhile, and we don't have the money for gas. I am sorry none of you could make it to Susie's wedding, which is, of course, another reason we are short of cash. The boy is named Roy Pucket, and he is shipping out, so they wanted to get married before he left. He is a friend of Buddy's from basic training and is a very nice boy. Susie is following him directly. I am glad Buddy got to see you on his leave. It sure will be different around here without them kids.

Your loving daughter, Rose Hartle.

Dear Violet,   September 17, 1950

Well, I will be coming on the bus a week come Monday. I want to tell you that Joe has left. He got himself a girlfriend. I know he picked her up in some bar. What kind of a woman would go off with a married man? We have lost everything. There is nothing left after these four years of hard work. On my part anyway. Susie's baby is a boy named Luke after Roy's father. Susie is back. Don't tell Mama how old that baby is. I hope you thank the Lord sometimes that you never had kids to give you such troubles. Mama can't remember nothing anyway. Buddy and his wife are stationed out on the West Coast. I never met her. But she is a Yankee.

Your sister, Mrs. J. L. Hartle.

Dear Susie,   October 4, 1950

I can't tell you how much you hurt me taking in your no-good father and that tramp of a woman friend of his. His own no-good family won't even have nothing to do with him. You was wrong if you thought I wouldn't find out. If you want to hear only one side of the story and that is his side, good riddance to you. I done everything I could for you, even to lying to your poor grandmother for you. And this is the thanks I get. Thank you anyway for the picture of my grandbaby. Maybe you will let me see him sometime.

Your hurting mother, Mrs. J. L. Hartle.

Dear Buddy,   November 1, 1950

Well, this is your mother writing you from your grandmother's. I don't know what kinds of stories you have heard from others

in the family. But your father has turned out worse than your grandfather. Either one of them. So I warn you to watch out for the drink, or it will get you, too. I hope you and your family is fine. Tell your nice wife I am real pleased to be a grandma again. I am not going to be here for good. I am going into town for a place of my own. It is no good living with relations. I hope I can find me a job because there is nobody to take care of me. At least I did not count on my daughter. Your Aunt Violet and Uncle George is back in town, and I can stay with them until I can get on my feet. Don't be like your selfish sister and take sides in family business. You are lucky to be so far away from this mess. I wish I was.

Your loving mother, Mrs. Rose Hartle.

Dear Mama,   January 6, 1951

It was nice to see you looking so good. I know you will miss Pa, but I hope not too much. I do not know why a family wants to be so mean at funerals. It was none of my dear sister's business if I had a man friend. And that is over now anyways. She should not judge anybody. The way she and George carry on. They are pretty common with their drinking and hanging around in bars. I do not need her or my children telling me how to live. Your precious Buddy gets his stories from his sister, and neither of them kids has ever did nothing for me, which I can say I did for them. I should be let to live my own life. And the dead should be left in peace. I will miss Pa, too, even though I never got on too good with him. God bless his soul.

Your loving daughter, Rose Hartle.

Dear Susie,   January 14, 1951

Well, I guess I just have to eat my words. Thank you for the $10.00. Pride goes for a fall, they say. And I do need it. You know your father never give me a cent. It was good to see you at your granddaddy's funeral. And little Luke. He is so cute. I never rode in an airplane, even when your father was in the service. You kids are lucky, nowadays. I am sorry about you and Roy, and him being no good, too. You can see how I have ended up with your father turning out bad. Maybe there is something good to be said for divorce though I never thought I would see the day when I would think that. But your father won't give me one because he don't want to have to support me. Please write me here in care of the Sweet Light Mission. Thank you again, and God bless you.

Your mother, Mrs. Rose Hartle.

Dear Violet,   March 7, 1953

Well, our paths do cross. There you are at home again and me here in town. I want you to know how good the Sweet Light Mission people has been to me. I never thought much of any of that, but I know better now. They did want me to join their army for God, and don't you think that is pretty funny after all my years as an army wife and mother? I am too weak to join, and I can't find the time. They give me stamps for my letters. I am sorry about George's accident. That old devil alcohol was driving poor George's car that night. It don't seem like it's been two years since Pa died. But it is time to let bygones be bygones. I know you are sorry for the way you treated me, and I am sorry for what I have done. I get my meals here at the Mission. God bless you and Mama, and I pray every day for George to walk and talk again.

Yours in the name of the Sweet Lord, Mrs. Rose Hartle.

Dear Buddy,   September 1953

Now that your grandmother is dead and gone I have no one left but my children and my dear sister. God bless you all. I am real busy, and I get around this town a lot. Thank you for the coat. I wear it every day, and I can turn it inside out when the weather changes for the good. Sister Clara told me she wrote you that I was in need. God bless you. Yours in the name of the Lord. Your loving and devoted mother,

Sister Rose Hartle.

Dear Violet,   January 1954

It is true what I told you that you haven't changed a bit, only gotten older. I was sorry we couldn't go to my place for Xmas dinner, but it is being fixed up. Don't they fix a nice do at the Mission though? And the breakfast you treated me to was real fine. God bless you. Amen. When you come again, you can find me in the same place or real close by. Or you can ask Captain Smith. She keeps track of me and my comings and goings. My legs are bad, so I sit more than I used to. Also, I have too much to carry far. I sing in the chapel on Sunday. Thank you and thank the Good Lord for being so generous. And for my dear sweet children. I hope you will visit me the next time you visit George. If he was to be able to recognize me, I would visit him myself. I sure wish you and George had come out to Friendly Acres. We could have had real good times. God bless you always.

Your loving sister, Sister Rose Hartle.

The Life and Death
of Martha

Every night I come home, my ankles is as purple as them onions in Mr. Strata's market. It's the one on the corner. He give me one once, said it was Spanish. I thought he was Italian. My feet hurt so bad I soak 'em in Epsom salts. Every night, it's like that, six nights a week. That's 'cause I work six days. I got the day shift. The night shift pays better. But I can't work nights 'cause I can't stay awake. I tried. The union let me. I been there a long time, and they said I could. But it was too much for me. I need my rest. I been sleeping nights all my life.

Mr. Strata says they got oranges in Italy that is purple and red. Blood oranges, they call 'em. Like the blood from the heart of Jesus on Mr. Strata's wall. He's a Catholic, Mr. Strata, but he's a friend to me.

I lift trays all day. Lift 'em and stack 'em. Six days. Saturday, we get out early. It's a short day. I visit my neighbor upstairs. She's very old, I guess, and she needs company. I go see her other times, too. On Sundays, in the morning. Mostly every day I come home and soak my feet in salts, and I think about what I done during the day. Not about trays. Maybe about what some joke somebody told. I try to remember it. Or what one of the fellows said to me. They're nice. They don't stack. That's what us women do. The fellows, they push them way-high tray stacks to the next room. The floors is all cement, and the wheels on the stacks is rubber. They roll real smooth. Them men laugh and ask how my feet is. I say good, fellows. That's what I call 'em, fellows. Sometimes one of the other women who stacks, like Ginger, she says, how's it going? So I say, how's the kids? On break time we stop in front of our trays,

and they talk. They talk about money or husbands. Sometimes I tell them about my neighbor, Mrs. Lubell. I say she's old and lonely, and I go up to see her. They tell me it's real good she has me to visit her. She don't have family, I say. And they ask me about my feet. My feet has always been bad, I guess.

*   *   *

My sister Martha was a very simple person. It ain't always the truth, sweet and simple. She was stingy, and she could be mean. She never liked my kids, never did for them. There she was, all by herself, and me with those kids and my troubles and all I did for her. So you think for one minute that she ever offered to help me and them kids out? No, sir. I asked her how she spent her wages. She was tighter than a chigger to a hound with what she had, which was not much, but she says to me she is putting it away for insurance to go to me. Well, money way ahead did me no good, 'cause she also says she wants a nice funeral, the works. There ain't enough in that policy for no fancy funeral, and insurance don't pay right off, so that's why she had to go to the city lot. Which is good anyway, 'cause that's where our mama is. And I'll go, most likely. So she took it to her grave, Martha did, and it's gonna take so long to get it, and my kids are pretty much grown, so it ain't gonna put no food on my table.

I said she was simple. She was so simple she never found nobody to look after her, so she did work herself to death if you ask me. She worked in that crummy plant for years, and they didn't do nothing for her. They didn't help out with the burial, nothing. Those great friends of hers, you think I heard a word from a one of them? No, sir.

I tried once to get her to move near me. This neighborhood is gone down. But she wouldn't hear nothing of it.

She never even learned to ride the bus. That's how slow she was. Didn't even want to. Family is family, so I come to see her.

Believe me, I did all I could for her. And look what I get. Some two-bit insurance policy that I got to track down, and I bet they won't even pay. I bet she was had good when she took it out.

*   *   *

I always worked since I left school. My first work was in a mill. Doing piecework. But I was too slow. When we moved to town, that's when I went to work. I was raised up in the country, but my daddy never had his own place, and we shifted a lot. So I got that mill job, then this one. It was my sister who always helped me, my baby sister. She visits me. Some Sundays she comes and sits in that chair, and we talk. I boil up some coffee, I always keep it for company, and we talk about when we were kids or how she is doing. Our folks is dead now. There were more of us, two sisters and a brother, but they moved on. Lil, she tries to fix me up. Do my hair and stuff.

I live here on the third floor. I climb them stairs every night, six nights a week, but I don't hardly go out on Sundays. It's too much for me. For two years I've had this radio, and I listen to it on Sunday. They read the funny papers on it. I don't listen the rest of the week. I don't forget on Sunday 'cause I say to myself, well, it's Sunday, what you gonna do before your company and your visiting, and I remember the radio. On Saturday I go to Mr. Strata's on the way home and get my groceries. He likes to teach me about things, like about the onions and the blood in the oranges. He gives me funny vegetables. Cook this, he says, just put a little oil and garlic in and cook it up. You'll love it. I don't always love it, but I thank him. I don't keep no garlic. I just put it in a pot with water and boil it. Some things I don't like he gives me, I give them to Mrs. Lubell.

My sister Lil found this place for me. I been here so long I can't hardly remember when I got here. It's my place. It's what I need. I share a bathroom, like when I was coming up. Lil, she has her own place. Most people in this building been here a long time. We're all neighbors now.

I seen all the changes on this street. All the cars, no more ice wagon. I can't get down the stairs in time to get from

The Life and Death of Martha

*   *   *

My baby sister, Lil, she visits me. Our folks is dead. On her days off, Sundays. I give her my best chair and boil coffee, like I said, I always keep it for good, and we talk. She has a good job. She works counter at a five and ten cent store, selling hairpins and such. It takes her maybe an hour to come see me 'cause she has to transfer. She is real good to me. She don't bring her kids. They make me nervous. I love 'em, but I worry 'cause I don't know how to act with 'em. They used to tease me, be mean to me. Lil says she brought 'em up right. She don't know why they act like they do. She don't want them to come anyway, 'cause she likes to get away by herself. And I'm family, so she comes to see me. Sometimes she brings a loaf of store bread and lunch meat, and we make sandwiches. Maybe bologna. Or fancy loaf with red and green in it. I like that. She does her nails, and mine, too, when she feels like it. My hair, she did once, too.

On the way home from work, I stop and see everybody I know, which is most of them on the block. I visit the stores. I have all the time in the world. So on the way home I go in the stores, and people say, how's your feet? Mrs. Green has the store where I buy my company coffee and my canned goods. Her husband died. He drove a taxi. She says to me, I'm alone like you. I say to her, Mr. Green was a nice man. I don't tell her I forgot what he looked like. She gives me dented cans with no labels and says, it's a guessing game. I give 'em to you, she says, 'cause I hate to see waste, and I can't sell 'em. Have fun. That's what she says. So there's Mr. Strata and Mrs. Green and Mr. Goldman. They are my friends, besides my neighbor, Mrs. Lubell, and my baby sister.

*   *   *

I gave that woman canned goods, right out of my stock. I felt sorry for her. She did keep to herself, and she worked at that plant for years, and they don't pay a decent wage.

I was standing out there when the ambulance come. They send the same, ambulance or hearse. The same thing whether you're dead or dying. I see everything that goes on. Then these women around here, they start saying they heard the dead one was an old hooker. I never heard that in all the time she lived here. Well, I seen men on this street walking like they might have something like that on their minds. I am a widow, you know, so I know that look on a man. So, who knows, maybe she was hiding something. But ain't that a note, spreading stories when she ain't even in her grave yet?

I was generous with her. I thought, the poor thing, she don't have a soul in this world. She didn't even have a cat, like that crazy one that lives above her. There's a bunch of lulus in that building. Nothing surprises me. I seen a lot from this here door.

*   *   *

Lil, she helped me in school. I can read some. I was the oldest, but she was the smartest. When I was little, my mother kept me close to her, even if I wasn't the baby. We did all the food putting up, of course, and we did my daddy's work when he was laid up. He was bad to drink, sometimes. Plowing, planting, hoeing up, the two of us. The others hired out. That's the way it was. I never went to school till my sister helped me. My other sisters and brother, they moved on, up north, Lil says.

I make enough right here to pay my rent and buy food and salts and stockings. I wear them heavy ones. Mrs. Lubell told me to get them. I got bad feet. I got a good coat, had it ten years now. Lil helped me save for it. I got a radio. It was at the pawn shop. That's where Mr. Goldman is. I know him. He said, Martha, don't you want a radio? I got one for you. So he talked me right into it. I listen to the funnies. A quarter a week till it was mine. He gave me a special, Mr. Goldman did.

Once my sister asked me what I did with all my money. She said, you must be making plenty. I showed her my envelopes. I got every one. It's not so much, she said. She was surprised. I seen it on her face. Where does it go, she said. So I told her about my insurance. I told her I named her in it. She gets it when my time comes. She said that made her nervous. I laughed when she said that. She is my family, and she does for me. She'll see to me when it's my time. And she has a family of her own, too.

* * *

I give her a good price on a radio. So she starts coming in every day on her way home from the plant. Finally, I says to her, you keep the real customers away. She thought that was a riot. She smiles and says thank you. I knew she weren't all there, but I didn't know how bad off she was. She's back the next day, and the next. So finally I give up. Every day she stops by, smiles, says, "I'm keeping the regular customers away." What a character! Well, it's too bad, that's all I can say.

* * *

Mrs. Lubell, she sent the insurance man to me. That was more than a quarter a week. Not like the radio. The man teased me about getting married. Sometimes they tease me about that at work, too. My mama used to say, when I hurt myself or was crying, she'd say, it's gonna get better 'fore you get married. I never thought about it, getting married, and I got better anyway.

I don't think my mama died 'cause she worked so hard. And she was married to a mean man. That's what Lil says. But he never took to me, my daddy. She give me my own name, my mama did. I'm not named after no one else, just me. The rest, he made her name them after his family people.

When I die, my sister is going to give me a real funeral. With lots of bought flowers. But I am going to be around for a while. I know. I had my fortune told once. There was an old gypsy, in that store two blocks over. The little one where they sell hot dogs now. My sister and me, we went to see her. On a Sunday. And she read our palms. She said I would live long and happy, and that Lil would, too, but Lil would have her troubles. Lil said she already had plenty of troubles.

When I think of dying, I say my prayers. That's the thing to do. Preachers always taught me that. Up close that old gypsy smelled like when we used to work fields, like fresh dirt. That's a right good smell.

So I go to work, and I take care of myself. I soak my feet and visit my friends. Mrs. Lubell reads the Bible to me every Sunday morning. After the funnies go off, it's time to go up and see her. I like the sound, but I don't understand the words. My mama read it, too. Mrs. Lubell has a little voice, and I always think she's going to start crying when she reads. She says it's her duty. Sometimes she says, what do you think about, Martha? And I tell her, I don't know, how am I supposed to know what I think? Then she tells me about Mr. Lubell and how she misses him. God Rest His Soul, all the time she says that. He's been gone since before I came here.

What I think about, I guess, is things I see out my window. It's right on the street. And about my sister, Lil. My friends, my supper, that's what I think about. The fellows at the plant, and the ladies, too. My feet. I think about good things, mostly. Remember good times, that's what me and Lil do. She says, always remember the good times. And we had some. When we were little, before we started shifting. We had a grandmother, on my mama's side she was, and she always said she would be happy if she could be buried where she was born. I want to die and be buried here, where I belong, she said. That is the way God meant it, she said. I wish I could die there, too, 'cause I was born on her place. And we always had good times there.

*　　*　　*

I had a mass said for her, bought a candle. Now I'm getting the real blood oranges in, sweet and ripe, and she won't get to see them. I pray for her soul.

*　　*　　*

But I'm still living, and I got my friends and my sister. Lil fixes my hair sometimes when she comes. Cuts it and washes it. She loves to mess with hair. She always curls her hair with bobby pins and wears a rag on her head. She put mine in pins once, but it fell. She said the curl didn't take. It hurt, too, pulled at my head.

So. I say my prayers at night, on my knees, every night of the week. And I soak my feet when I come home, six nights a week. And I work all day. That's what I do. That's my life.

Bar Song

He packed the beer cans into the full bag and picked it up. When he got to the door, he set the bag down and took the top four cans out. He put them in the garbage can, between TV-dinner trays and an empty cigarette carton, then stood back and appreciated the arrangement: four for the landlady to see, the rest for the dump.

Three o'clock. Three hours into a new day. He shoved the screen door open with his hip and put the bag down while he lit a cigarette. A white police cruiser went through the intersection at the bottom of the hill. It turned around in the supermarket parking lot and went back the way it had come.

Three was the still, quiet time. The bars closed at two, and by three the drunks had gone home. Before three, cars passed and horns honked. At four, good people would be getting up for the five or six o'clock shift, the drunks passed out in their beds, or someone else's bed, or in an alley. Or standing on the porch, smoking. He flicked the cigarette into the bushes and watched until the orange spot had faded. By five, there was light above the supermarket roof, the streetlights out. At five, a German shepherd on the next block would start barking.

An ambulance drove by, lights flashing. He pushed the bag across the porch with his foot, then sat down on the top step and pulled the bag to him. The ambulance was headed downtown, to the big hospital. Maybe there was some poor bum in the back, somebody who hadn't learned to drink at home and leave the bars alone. He had tried a song about that, about being a drunk and learning the hard way to stay home. One more song, and he'd be on top again. One good hit, that, and the only hit he'd ever seen, his big one, the biggest of the year, then. Every time that song came to mind, he cried. He hugged the bag to his chest.

A light went on in the upper window of the big brown house across the street. Three-fifteen, or right about then. He'd never passed a three-fifteen when that light hadn't come on. He lit another cigarette and held it in the corner of his mouth as he started down the steps. The smoke burned his eyes, and he felt ahead for each step as he set a foot down. He had tried to make a song about that light, but there were too many songs about night watches like his, about crying in the night, about coming home from bars at three in the morning.

Bars. had been about as good to him as his bar songs had been. They never made the charts, barely got air time. More lost than gained in bars: he'd lost his teeth, his women, his money, his pride. No credit for him anymore, hell, no teeth. A man with four teeth in his mouth can't very well sit at the bar and grin and laugh and buy rounds, especially when those four teeth are all that man has got left.

He stood on the sidewalk and watched a red car go through the intersection, so fast it was a blur of sound. Probably young kids, in college, maybe, their lives ahead of them. No school could teach how to write songs. Songs, they say, come from the heart. His songs had, right from his ignorant God-loving heart. But his heart was no fool. He and his heart had sung in bars, in clubs, at the Opry. And then he made his own songs, right from the heart and soul. Where was that heart now, giving him nothing but noise in the ears like the blur of noise from the red car, pounding in his soul and keeping him from rest. My heart is a red car, going nowhere in the night, an old red heart. Heart songs.

The old gray Chevy and he had gotten to look alike, drab and used. He opened the door and pushed the front seat forward. The bag fit under the army blanket, against the row of bags on the seat, on top of the bags on the floor. The back was almost full, about up to the windows. There was room for four or five more bags, four or more days, if he packed them in good and tight. Count your beer cans one by one, and see what you have done. He would take the trip to the dump, sure it would be the Chevy's last as he would nose her along in the far right lane, would push her hard to get up to twenty.

The light across the street was out. He ground the cigarette in the gutter and stood with his hands in his pockets. Downtown, the clock chimed once, three-thirty. Two miles to the courthouse clock, straight downtown to bright lights, night spots and fun, the boulevard of dreams. There were hundreds of songs, good ones, about that road to success, to Music Row, to money and love. It was the road to hell, the boulevard of broken dreams.

He looked up the street, into the shadows of spring leaves, then down to the intersection and the yellow blinking light, the supermarket and vacant lot, the out-of-business filling station. One day it stayed closed, and there was a sign on the door, "Sorry, We're Closed," and under it in purple crayon, "for good." Things went that way. Here one day pumping gas, washing road dirt off windshields, gone the next, and nobody cares or knows where or why.

My heart is a vacant lot without your love. He walked up the stairs, stopping on each one, and got another beer. My heart is a filling station with no gas. He sat on the top step, lit another Lucky, and opened the beer. Next week, he would empty the car, start over. Shave, clean up, take a walk downtown. Walk into Tootsie's, cool and serious. Somebody sees him, yells, hey, see what we got here, and the lead guitar of the pickup band nods his way while the band starts up on the refrain chords of his songs, and everybody sings along, lifts drinks in his direction. Where you been keeping, they say, and a young kid looks at him with respect, admiration, and buys him a real drink and then slips a ten—no, a twenty—into his back pocket.

Tears work their way down his face. He holds the beer high, and, with his other hand, he covers his heart. The applause throbs behind his ribs, and the noise in his ears becomes a jubilant roar, until his body shakes with it, and, as he falls, he hears a siren.

Amy Rose, 1947

She sat outside the store on a crate to one side of the screen door, hands folded, ankles crossed, feet dirty. Her white hair was pushed behind her ears, and her face and dress were lined with dust. She was almost six, and she squinted in the strong sunlight. Around at the side of the store, her father laughed and drank with the other men. Her mother had stayed at their new place, asleep.

In front of the gas station, two rusting pumps leaned out of the cracked cement. The store sold cellophane-wrapped cakes, gum, chaw and snuff and cigarettes, Coca-Cola and RC, molasses and cornmeal. The whole building was made of tin—the roof hung over the edge of the door like a porch, the rolling walls wrapped around the sides. Under the roof's eave was the only shade. The heat made the air smell like hot tar, gasoline, dust.

The night before, long after dark, her father met them. Amy Rose and her mother Anne were the only ones to get off, the only white people left on the bus. JD took them to his rooms in the bottom of a big, old house. He carried Amy Rose over his shoulder, and she remembered his smell. JD and Anne had a bed in the back room, and Amy Rose slept on a folded blanket under the kitchen table. The toilet was in a small closet with a pull chain too high for her to reach. The kitchen had a single tap that ran cold water all the time. The rooms were musty and damp.

Amy Rose had gotten up early and gone outside, around to the front of the house. She stood under a tree in its heavy, sweet smell, looking at the red dust road. The ground was covered with small, pink, feathery mimosa fans, and she picked one up and brushed the fluffy end across her lips. She went back in the door as her father came out of the bathroom, zipping his fly. He put a pan of water on the hot plate.

"We'll go out, when I have this coffee, and I'll find you some breakfast. Then I gotta take care of some dogs. Little ones. You might like to see 'em. Puppies, they are."

The door to the back room was closed. They left Anne asleep.

JD and Amy Rose went around the corner of the house and across the dirt road, up the shoulder of the tar road toward the store. The air shimmered around the gas pumps. JD lit a cigarette and pushed his hair back. He was bold and short, strong, her mother said, from his deals and ordeals.

He walked in front. "Don't go near the road," he said. "It'll burn your feet. Walk in the dust." In the road, the heat rose, and the tar bubbled.

Three men were in front of the store, two of them leaning under the eaves, one sitting in a crate. His body seemed to be folded against the tin wall.

"Hey, JD, what the hell is that? Yours is it? Do it look like you?" He laughed and poked the men standing next to him.

"Watch your mouth. Giver her that seat, Nason. I got to get her some breakfast. Her Mama's still in the bed."

Nason unfurled his long, slack body, and JD pushed Amy Rose toward the crate. She sat down carefully, tucking her dress under her to protect her legs from splinters. Sweat dissolved the dust at her temples, and her whole scalp felt itchy. Her dress was the one she had slept in on the bus. She wanted a clean one, wanted to change her clothes and wash up.

The men followed JD into the store. Amy Rose sat looking across the road at a shack, a house with too many corners. It sloped down on one side and was propped up with cinder blocks on the other. Chickens with no feathers on their tails pecked near the black strip of road. They pecked in circles, raising puffs of dust. A rabbit pen was off to one side. Its wire mesh bottom sagged to the ground. The rabbits hopped from shade to shade. Behind the house and to both sides were the pines, stretching back and on down the road, going out of town and on without end. A biddy took a dust bath near the stoop of the house. It was quiet except for the noise from inside the store and the chickens cursing the rabbits. Amy Rose did not know what day it was, only that it was her first day at this new home.

JD came out and handed her a grape soda and a cellophane-wrapped package. He took the cake back, unwrapped it, and gave it back to her.

"Here. And you'd best eat every bit. Your mama says you don't eat good."

The dry cake made her gag. She put her mouth over the top of the bottle, but the soda pop smell was not like real grapes. She took small bites of cake followed by fast swallows of drink. Then she set the bottle at her feet beside the wrapper and folded her hands.

A green, patchy-looking truck came slowly from the point of the pines. It stopped beside the store. A man got out, and a big boy jumped over the tailgate. They looked at Amy Rose and went into the store. The noise inside grew, then they all came out, five men and the boy. The store owner was an old man, his face blurred like the words on a gravestone. His overalls made him look long and narrow, and his hands appeared to hang to his knees. The other men were younger and wore khaki pants and T-shirts left over from the army. One had tattoos covering both his arms. The T-shirts were rusty in the creases and armpits. The big boy was wearing dungarees and a long-sleeved flannel shirt. The holes in his pants showed ugly, gray knees. He hopped into the bed of the truck.

"Get that sack," someone said. "We ain't got all day!" The men laughed and echoed, "We ain't got all day. Sure. What the hell you got to do? Check's done come already!" One spit from the corners of his mouth, tobacco juice sliding out with his words.

"You stay put," JD told Amy Rose. "I'll show you one of them puppies. Gimme one."

The boy handed a burlap bag to one of the men, who pulled out a brown and white puppy and gave it to JD. He put it into Amy Rose's lap. She picked it up and held it belly-side up, like a doll.

"It's real cute. Can I have one?"

"Well, for a time. But I got to train it to hunt. Then I'll have to take it back. It won't be no good for playing with. Not if it's to be a good hound. Right now, we're gonna fix them up. We don't want no hounds with stringy tails. Give it here. You want more to eat?"

She handed him the puppy and shook her head. "No, sir."

"Set then, and behave."

The men and the boy walked around the corner to the side of the store. The first day was already long, and she hoped she could find her way back to her mother, to the house, if her father left her. She knew the smell of whiskey that the men were drinking. Her father always left when he was drinking.

Around the corner the men sniggered and laughed, the dogs yipped and moaned. She heard a single yelp, then a series of high sharp cries. She got up and walked close to the corrugated walls, one hand running over the humps. The dust was silky powder under her feet and made perfect footprints behind her. Holding on to the wall, she peeked around the sharp, tin side.

Two of the men sat on wide steps leading to the store's side door. Her father was one of them. The other men leaned against the truck. JD held a puppy in his hand. With the other hand, he wrapped a handkerchief around the pup's tail, then put the tail in his mouth and bared his teeth as he bit. The dog's cry rose in fast, high-pitched yelps. JD took the bloody cloth away from his mouth and shook something from it into a pail at the bottom of the steps, then rinsed the cloth in another bucket full of dark pink water. One of the men took the dog and swabbed the stump with coal tar.

She threw up. It spewed out of her mouth, through her fingers, onto the ground. The purple stream missed the skirt of her dress, landed beyond her toes. The big boy pointed and JD turned around. He got up, grabbed her by the arm, and pulled her back around to the crate, scraping her legs on its edges as he pushed her down. He went into the store and came out with a wet, gray rag. He wiped her hands and mouth. She was crying.

"Stop that. I told you to stay put! You sick?"

She choked and tried to stop, holding her breath. Her face

was wet and gritty, and she wanted to wipe the smell of the greasy rag off. Her head and shoulders jerked with each breath. JD pulled her back to her feet, then lifted her into the crook of his arm. He shoved dirt over the mess with his foot, then walked back around to the steps and sat her down.

"This is for they own good. It don't hurt really, just surprises them a little. Their tails got to be docked. Now you look here, and you'll see how it's done, then you won't get upset." He took a clean rag and put it in her hand. Then he guided her fingers up the tail of the next puppy, to the end. He pinched down. "That's the last joint, where it gots to come off clean."

She pulled her hand free and put both hands between her knees. She had hiccups.

JD picked up the finished dog and handed it to her. She sat still. "You take it," he said.

She took the puppy, its tail smeared with pitch, dirt, drying blood. One of the men handed her a bandana to put in her lap.

JD squatted and bounced a few times on his haunches, his sharp whiskey and tobacco breath in her face. He looked in her eyes and stuck his cigarette in his mouth. "Hey, sugar," he said, "it's all right."

*　　*　　*

Amy Rose named the puppy Baby. Back in the dark rooms, Anne sat at the table in her slip, smoking Pall Malls and reading a paperback. She pushed her long hair back and looked up at them over her coffee cup. JD stood in front of Amy Rose and the dog. Anne spoke to him in the tone she used when she explained something to Amy Rose.

"You know, there is no food in this dump, JD. Nothing but a bag of coffee. You knew we were coming. What the hell are we supposed to eat?"

"Good morning to you, too," he said. "I fed the girl." He shoved Amy Rose aside and walked out.

"Well, look at that. Ask him a simple question, and he walks out. Can't take it already. And he's been drinking, too. Nothing changes. Oh, no food in this hole, but he got his little girl a puppy. What's wrong with that animal's behind?" She walked to the door and stood with her hands on her skinny hips.

"Tails got to be docked," Amy Rose said.

"Have, not got. I can't win. Not between him and my mother. We got to live somewhere. He walks out, she runs her mouth."

Anne dressed in the back room while Amy Rose and Baby watched.

"Your grandmother has got you fooled, little girl. It's her fault we had to come back to him. She pushes, just keeps at me about him. Sure, he's going to change. I'm stuck again, that's what." She started through the kitchen to the door. "I'm going to get some food. You wait here, and don't let that dog make a mess. Don't let anybody in." She walked back and kissed Amy Rose, then left.

When Amy Rose and Baby awoke from their nap, Anne was back at the table in her slip. Amy Rose took the puppy outside, and, after it squatted and peed, she picked it up and petted it, whispering, "Good dog, good Baby," into the pink of its ear.

They had chicken noodle soup and saltines, and Amy Rose put her bowl down for the puppy to lick. Then she washed in the sink and changed into clean clothes.

They went out for a walk, but it was so hot they stopped. They sat under a pine, avoiding its oozing pitch. Amy Rose put her head down on the puppy, rubbed her lips back and forth on the soft ear and face. The puppy smelled like her own warm skin and something else, maybe wet dirt. The tail had a hard crust on it, and she was careful not to touch it.

Anne pulled Amy Rose to her, put the child's head in her lap. "You are the only good to come from the war. Now I got no job, a no-good husband, a mama who still wants to tell me how to live my life. You know what? I'm between the devil and a rock. But don't you think about it. I'll always take care of you. And even your daddy is nice to you. You got that dog."

They sat under the tree in the heat of the afternoon, and, when the sun had moved and a small breeze went through the tree above them, they stood, and Anne brushed the dry pine needles from them both. They walked back along the shoulder of the road to the store. She left Amy Rose on the crate and went off with one of the men to find JD.

Amy Rose watched the sun turn the color of orange Nehi, then Cheracol syrup, before Anne and JD returned. They bought groceries, then led Amy Rose and Baby back to the basement rooms.

Amy Rose sat outside the screen door, listening to crickets and watching. Anne stood at the table, making sandwiches while JD watched her, a beer in his hand, sitting with his back against the wall. He put his cigarette on the edge of the table and moved his hand up Anne's leg, under her slip.

"Annie, honey, you told your mother where to send your check, didn't you?"

Anne had a piece of white bread in one hand, the kitchen knife, yellow with mustard, in the other.

"Don't call me Annie. I did. How about you? Been looking for work, have you?"

The check and work made Amy Rose cover her ears. JD got up and walked to the door. He stood over her with his beer in one hand, the other hand in his pocket. She held her breath and took her hands away from her ears, but left them at the sides of her head.

"JD, don't go. I didn't mean anything. Here, your cigarette's burning the table." Anne dropped the knife and handed JD the cigarette. Amy Rose breathed in and out as he turned and sat back down.

They had sandwiches and buttermilk and cookies for supper. JD told Anne that he would be getting a car, would take her and the girl for a ride, would look for work. It was her allotment check, he didn't want none of it. He agreed to try again, to stay with them and make a real go of it. After supper, he and Anne left Baby and Amy Rose and went outside to sit in the cooling air.

Amy Rose woke to hear them laughing when they came in the door, and they bent over, each kissed her, and told her that they really were going to get along better, she should go back to sleep and be happy.

*   *   *

In the next few weeks they moved three times: a large place, lighter than the basement, with no furniture at all; a nice place where they were asked to leave after a late night fight; and finally, to the next town, where they rented a second-floor set of rooms in Anne's maiden name.

Letters came from Anne's mother up north. She sent a dollar to Amy Rose, to spend on herself, and a special letter:

> Dearest Amy: It has only been a month, but it seems like so much longer. I hope you are having a good time with your mother and father. I miss you, and you can come back to live with me anytime because I love you so very much. Your mother writes me that down there the magnolias are in full bloom. Do you like them? I bet you can read some of this yourself because you are my smart, sweet little girl. Love, Grandmother.

Amy Rose read her name. Anne wrote what she asked her to: she missed her grandmother, too, the flowers were very pretty, and her daddy got her a puppy named Baby.

Anne smoked, read, wrote letters to her girlfriends. She and Amy Rose went for long walks down dirt roads, made visits to the five and ten. With the dollar they bought red nail polish and candy: Sugar Babies, licorice shoe strings, watermelon candy, and a roll of Necco wafers. They slept inside in the noon heat.

JD was gone most nights and every day. He was looking for work, he said. Between dusk and dark he sat on the stoop with Amy Rose. He threw stones, and the puppy chased them. Sometimes Anne sat with them. When it was cool enough to sleep, he took Amy Rose in to bed and said, "Good night, my little sugar."

Baby learned to come to her name and followed Amy Rose and Anne. Anne talked as they walked.

"This, honey, is what your grandmother means when she says poor white trash. No food in the kitchen. Husband and daddy off carrying on, no thought to his wife and little girl.

Gambling, drinking. But I been good for him. It's hard on a man when he marries up. He's lucky he even met as good as me. He's better than the last time, honey. Really he is."

They sat on the bench in front of the hardware store, eating Popsicles and waiting for rain. Amy Rose licked the edges of a pink Necco wafer. Anne turned Amy Rose's face up to her own.

"I thought you'd be the difference in him, really I did. You being bigger, fun to play with. Men don't like babies. I figured he'd see us as a real family, and he'd straighten out."

Anne said the same things to JD when he was around. She told him she'd leave again if he didn't find work, stay to home. One evening, after he had slept through the day, she called him a mean bastard. He got up from the table and hit her in the face, his big hand splitting her lip. On the way out, he said, "Keep it to yourself, woman. And why in the hell don't you ever fix yourself up?"

Anne sobbed and moaned, her hands over her mouth. She rinsed the blood away and held an ice cube wrapped in a T-shirt to her lip, then took Amy Rose and the puppy into her lap. The cold water dripped down Amy Rose's arm, but she didn't move.

Two days later JD came back, and Anne was still angry. She screamed at him again: he was no good, she was leaving. He took her shoulders and shook her. Her head jerked back and forth, and her mouth hung open. Amy Rose hid her face in the dog's body in her lap. She felt its bones, its heart beating. JD walked out but came back an hour later. He was feeling sorry, he said. "I got a temper, you know that," he said to Anne. "Why can't you stay off my back? You push me too far. What else can I do?"

He wanted to make it up to them. He'd take them for a ride like he had promised and show them the country. "You all been cooped too long, you need some good air."

The next morning Anne led Amy Rose around the sunny kitchen in a jitterbug as she made a picnic lunch, fancy pimiento loaf sandwiches. She put them into a bag with cans of potato sticks, Coca-Cola and beer, and Moon pies for dessert. JD cooked them a real breakfast, grits and eggs and sausage. He held Amy Rose in his arms, so she could reach the pan and stir the grease and flour for gravy.

Midmorning, they left, Amy Rose and Baby in the rough plush back seat. They leaned on the armrest, Amy Rose up on her knees to see out the window.

Up front, Anne sat close to JD, and they laughed. It had rained the night before, and the road was puddles and mud, the dust changed to rusty soup. They drove down the main road and out the other side of town. Amy Rose and Baby put their heads out the window, and the wind blew Amy Rose's hair around her face while the hot air caught her breath.

Anne turned around and shouted, "Isn't this a good time, honey?" Amy Rose smiled and nodded. "We're going to get us a car, soon as your daddy gets steady work."

They drove through a colored town and past a cemetery of tall trees and small gravestones. Anne was talking to JD, but the air caught the words, carried them out the window. Then JD shouted, and Amy Rose turned to the front.

Anne had moved. She sat against the door. She shouted at JD, and the car went faster. JD made the car speed up and slow down, jerking it up the road. Up front, past the windshield, Amy Rose saw the black vee of the pines ahead where the rows of trees came together in the distance. They drove into the vee, without getting any closer to its end.

JD reached across the seat and grabbed Anne's hair, and she put her hands on the top of her head. Inside the car, everything went slow, while the road went faster and faster beneath them. Amy Rose cried, and Baby jumped against the front seat barking. She growled and grabbed JD's shoulder.

When JD hit the brakes, Amy Rose fell forward into the seat back, and the puppy was thrown to the floor. JD opened the door, grabbed the yelping dog, then threw it into the muddy ditch. He got back in and turned the car around in the middle of the road, driving fast again.

Anne screamed at JD that he was crazy.

"Get off my goddamned back! Nothing I do satisfies you."'

Amy Rose howled, her mouth wide open. Her head hurt.

Amy Rose, 1947

She balled up the skirt of her dress and put it in her mouth, holding it there with both fists. Anne climbed over the back seat to her and held her, the way Amy Rose had held the puppy, her face pressed against Amy Rose's back, her hair covering the child's heaving shoulders.

In front of the house, JD opened the car door. "I've had it. Go on home to your mama, Miss Goddamned Uppity Lady." He threw the picnic in the dirt and got back in the car. "I believe I'm as straightened out as I'll ever be." He drove off and splashed mud on Amy Rose and Anne.

The dishes from breakfast were still in the sink. Amy Rose sat in a kitchen chair and screamed, "I want my puppy! Give it back!" Anne pulled the dress over her head and threw it in the trash. The skirt was full of little holes where it had been chewed. She washed Amy Rose's face.

"It's my fault, honey. I am real sorry about your puppy. Things got too much for your daddy. I didn't give him enough time. That's what it is. We won't tell your grandmother all what happened, 'cause it would hurt her. We don't want to do that, do we?"

"I want my dog."

"Well, you couldn't have a dog at your grandmother's anyway."

Amy Rose watched her mother's back at the sink, heard the plates fall against each other in the drainer, smelled the sausage and gravy. When Anne was finished, they both slept.

Anne packed, and they left. Amy Rose eased her small black suitcase along, resting it on the side of her foot and pushing it ahead in the damp dirt.

Anne called her mother from a pay phone, collect. She and Amy Rose waited outside a filling station, sitting on their suitcases underneath a Coca-Cola sign. The owner brought over an old colored man and directed him to give the woman and child a lift to the bus stop.

They rode in the front seat of the jalopy, down the tar road that stretched again out through the pines, and back to the tin store.

Anne gave the old man a dime and thanked him. The crate

Amy Rose had sat on was empty. She sat down, and Anne brought them Dixie cups, then sat on the suitcases.

"Where do you think Baby is, Mama?"

Anne smoothed the hair from Amy Rose's forehead. "Don't you worry. She'll be all right. I bet he went directly back to her. That's what he was in such a hurry about, to get that dog. He wanted it for hunting, you knew that. Now that he doesn't have to look for work, why he'll be training it every day."

The air smelled like wet hens and more rain. Amy Rose looked down at her good shoes, the cracks in the patent leather fine as the feathers of the pink mimosa fans. Another slow truck came down the road. It passed by them, getting smaller and smaller until it blended into the pines.

Family Visit

Elma dipped the last plate into the dishwater and stared into the mirror above the sink, past her own thin face, at Vernon and the old lady. The old lady was rigid in her chair, arms straight out on the table in front of her. She sucked on her bottom lip and made wet, fleshy noises. Vernon sat across from her, eyes closed. He opened them and blew a wide, white smoke ring.

"Elma's got her mind set," he said.

"There is no reason on God's green earth why you can't go," Elma said. She lifted the dishpan and moved sideways out the door, then heaved the greasy water. Above its odor, the woods around gave the evening air the smell of wet pine and moss.

"If something was to come and carry off that pig or them stupid rabbits, you couldn't do nothing anyway." Elma stood in the doorway. "If there was even one reason—only one, mind you—then I wouldn't be set. Staying in this house for these nine years is no reason to keep staying in this house. I do not know how you can stand it." She dried her hands on her dress and, with the damp dish towel, wiped the table in wider and wider circles.

The old lady pushed her chair back and closed her hands into ropy fists. She leaned on them and rose, then moved stiff-legged into the bedroom. The foot of her cot faced the kitchen, and Elma kept an eye on her. "Don't you get into them clean sheets with your shoes on, or the rest of your things."

The old lady turned her back and, with wide motions, pulled off layer upon layer of clothing until she stood in stained knee-length drawers and a dirty vest. The pile at her feet came to the middle of her shins. She stepped out of it and got into bed.

The bedroom still smelled of wood smoke and the closed-in smell of winter and camphor. Elma tucked the covers in at the bottom of the girls' bed. They slept close together, Mabel on her side with an arm above her head, and next to her Betty had her thumb in her mouth and her suck rag in her fist. The old lady lay on her back, arms at her sides.

Vernon left the kitchen to sit on the porch and play his jaw harp. Elma gave the table a final swipe with her apron before she brought out the pattern and material for the girls' Easter dresses. The two views on the envelope showed a dark-haired child with sausage curls holding out the full skirt of a simple dress with a wide round collar, and a smiling, blonde Shirley Temple look-alike with a pinafore over the dress. Elma's girls bore no resemblance to either child, though she had wound Mabel's hair in rags to see if it would take, and, even with Nestle curl, the hair was still straight and fine.

She figured the changes for size, harder to do now that Mabel was taller, but still not much wider, than Betty. The material was a jonquil-yellow dotted swiss, with white piqué for the collar. Elma told that she made the girls' clothes because it was a saving; true, but, for more than a year, she had dressed them alike. They had been mistaken for twins more than once, and when they were, it followed that they were cute. It pleased them, and it was the only time they were given any notice.

One dress was pinned and both collars pinned and cut before Vernon came in. Elma put the pattern and material aside and started a list in the margin of the newspaper of what she had to do in the morning to get them off to an early start. She felt sure that she had forgotten nothing: dinner to get and pack, clean hankie, chewing gum in case her ears popped. She had to set her hair, so she would not be done until morning.

She stood in front of the mirror, wet the comb in a glass of water, and dampened small pieces of hair, then wound them in small tight circles and stuck two bobby pins into each curl. The kitchen stretched out behind her. She decided to move the long table. The old lady would have to walk all the way

Family Visit

'round it to get anywhere. The last time Elma had moved the table, Vernon had set it back when his mother asked him. But the old lady had gotten too stubborn to even ask. Even with the table turned, she would sit at her place, and, when Elma washed dishes, she would only have to see the broad back and ratty gray hair coming out of the hair net. Elma wrapped a terry-cloth turban around her pin curls and pulled the end of the table around.

*   *   *

The day was too hot too early, and the chatter of the katydids made it seem even hotter. Elma fried chicken and watched the first morning sunlight hit the shed door. It was her idea, this trip. She had put aside the money for gas and a treat on the way back, had marked the day on the calendar. It was time to do something, she told Vernon. She was tired of sitting around every weekend while he went out to drink beer and play cards with his friends, and she was stuck in the house. Vernon had not agreed to the visit, but he had not disagreed. It was for the girls, Elma said, for them to get to know Vernon's family, other than the old lady, and they would get to see a real TB hospital. It might teach them to take better care of themselves. There was a lot to be learned from such a trip.

*   *   *

Vernon came through the kitchen, his pants below his navel, two day's gray and brown stubble on his chin. He looked out the back door and scratched his bare chest, bowed and hard as a chicken breast. Elma stepped back from the popping grease and shook the last drumstick onto the almost transparent brown paper, which was piled with crisp chicken parts. She pulled the skillet from the fire and moved the coffeepot over the coals.

Outside, Vernon swirled water in his mouth and spit, then splashed. "Use the dipper," Elma yelled. "You are no example, Vernon George!" He splashed again. When he stepped through the screen door, Elma handed him the plate of sausage and a pitcher of cane syrup. She put the biscuits and sweet milk on the table.

Vernon sat down, a cup of coffee in front of him. Elma poked him with an elbow. "I done my part, mostly," she said. "Make her get in here, please."

Betty came out of the bedroom, thumb in mouth, pieces of her grandmother's clothing around her ankles. She leaned against her mother's knees. Elma turned her face up, and, with a piece of flannel, she wiped the sleep from Betty's eyes. "You can take a nap soon as you're in the car. Just eat and get dressed. That's all you got to do. All any of you got to do." She pulled Betty's thumb out, but it popped back in, so she worked around it to wipe away the thin, white crust at the corners of Betty's puckered lips.

Mabel was in her place. Elma pushed her chair in and lifted Betty onto the Sears Roebuck catalog. She served the girls' plates, then stood at her own place, her hands firm-set on the back of the chair. "Vernon. You get her to the table. We can't start till you do."

With his bare foot, Vernon nudged his mother's. He placed a hand on her shoulder and shook her. Her eyes opened. He nodded toward the table, then took her hand, pulled her to her feet, and guided her to her chair. She stood until he pushed her down.

Vernon bowed his head. "Amen. Maybe she don't like what you done with the table."

Mabel poured syrup over her plate and pushed her food around with a spoon. "This sausage is greasy."

Elma turned. "We don't need your opinion. Ten bites, or you stay to home."

Betty's thumb came out of her mouth with a loud, wet noise. "We can't stay home. You said nothing short of death was going to keep Grandma from going, and that means we don't have nobody to stay with us."

"I'll have to tie you to the porch, then, won't I?"

Betty's mouth opened wide, and the wrinkled, white thumb dropped below her chin.

"You know I'm just teasing, honey." Elma patted her tangled hair. "Looks like rats been nesting again." Betty smiled and showed tiny spaces where her baby teeth had been.

*   *   *

Elma fitted the chicken into a big bowl and set a plate over it, wrapped the biscuits in waxed paper, and fitted the dinner, along with two jars of cold tea, into the laundry basket, then set the basket on the porch. Mabel and Betty were following Vernon back from taking slop to the pig and feeding the rabbits. "We didn't get dirty, Ma, promise," Mabel said.

The old lady sat in front of her full plate. "Even the girls is helping," Elma said. She leaned over the old lady's shoulder. "I do not have time to put up with your nonsense," she whispered.

When the girls were dressed, Elma worked on Mabel's hair. "I hate this! I want short hair," Mabel said. She made fists in her lap, her back stiff as her grandmother's. "Don't think I don't know what you're doing." Elma tapped her head with the hairbrush. "Sit straight, or you'll look like some blind lady done you hair." She finished both sets of braids and tied green grosgrain ribbons around the ends, then sent the girls to sit on the porch.

Vernon sat at one end of the table, smoking, another cup of coffee in front of him.

"All right, Vernon. The girls are waiting. The dinner is packed. We will take your mother in her nightgown."

Vernon blew smoke rings and waited. His mother did not move. He brought his fist down on the table. The women started.

"Ah, shit." He and his mother stood at the same time. She was more than a head taller than he was. "Do it, Mama."

Elma looked at his dirty, shapeless T-shirt. "Aren't you going to get dressed?"

"Nope. It's my day off."

*   *   *

Elma's feet were up on the dashboard. She pulled thin strips of red enamel from her toenails and let them blow out the window. Vernon drove with one hand on the roof, the other arm around the steering wheel.

In the corner behind Vernon, the old lady sat with her arms twisted together so that her face rested on her folded hands. Her fat lower lip stuck out beyond her chin. The little girls were crowded together in the opposite corner of the wide seat. They refused to sit next to their grandmother. Mabel said she smelled like an old, pissy quilt.

Vernon stared straight ahead at dull, metal-gray clouds in front of them. "Bet I can make it through that rain."

The old lady made a slurping noise, and Elma turned around. "Mother, won't you be glad to see your girls?" She took the last two pins out of her hair and brushed her two-toned curls.

Mother did not open her eyes. "Nope."

"Well, why on earth not? I believe it's been more than ten years, way more."

"I don't need to see them. I know what they look like."

"Well, I don't. I'm looking forward to this. And the girls is, too."

The girls were awake and fighting for the window. Mabel elbowed Betty onto the floor, but Betty made a firm fist and socked her big sister in the back. Elma ignored them until Mabel landed a solid punch, and Betty gave up in sobs. "That's enough," Elma said, and Mabel let Betty have the window back.

"You never seen twins, have you?" Elma asked.

Mabel answered. "Only calves, once." Betty shook her head, her thumb solidly in her mouth.

"Well, I did," Elma said. "It was at a USO dance. You should have seen them men go wild. I hoped I might have twins. They run in families. Was your girls really identical, Mother?"

The old lady sucked on her bottom lip.

"I said, could they be told apart?"

"I ain't deef."

"They weren't hers," Vernon put in. "They were my daddy's."

"Well, that makes no difference. I asked a real question."

"They was alike as two snakes."

Mabel pulled herself forward until she was face to face with her mother. "Snakes! I don't want to see no snakes!" She leaned back and smiled.

Elma drew in her breath and narrowed her eyes, the look that said, "that's enough." "You know how your grandmother is. And she don't need help from your mouth, missy. She can be plenty testy on her own."

Vernon looked at his mother in the rearview mirror. "She ain't testy," he said. "She don't like to waste words. Plenty of people don't like to talk, but you wouldn't know 'cause you ain't one of them." He lit a cigarette and lifted his hip to put the lighter back in his pocket. Elma reached under him and took the lighter, then pinched him.

"Damn it, I am trying to drive, so stop fooling with me."

She tossed the lighter onto the dashboard. "And I am trying to have us a good time. You don't need to be so ugly. We got enough of that, too, without any help."

Mabel leaned over the front seat. "How long till our picnic? When we gonna get there?"

"Long enough," Elma said. "You heard your daddy. Don't talk so much. We'll stop when we see a decent place."

At the edge of a town, they slowed. The shoulders of the road became the front-yard patches of shacks. Old colored men under straw hats sat on their haunches or propped themselves against rotten porch posts. Further along, a group of colored children ran alongside the car. The curl rags in the little girls' hair bobbed like cabbage butterflies at the tops of their heads. In the center of town, in front of a gas station and post office, white men stood in the same lazy way the coloreds had.

Vernon stopped on the other side of the town. He pulled the Studebaker off the road, into the shelter of some pines. Elma spread the red gingham oilcloth over the dense, soft needles. The girls were dressed in their Sunday best, and Elma wore her traveling clothes, her next-best turquoise pedal pushers and white peasant blouse. She made the girls sit on the edge of the cloth to stay clean, and so they would have their backs to the old lady and her poor manners. The old lady refused to get out of the car and ate in her seat with the door open and her feet hanging out. She beat the biscuits with her bare gums and picked the chicken meat into pieces small enough to swallow whole.

Elma packed the leftovers and paper back into the basket and threw the crumbs and chicken bones into the woods. Vernon smoked, lying on his back in the front seat of the car, while Mabel and Betty walked along the ditch and picked ragged robin. They found a grasshopper, and it spit tobacco juice on Betty's dress. Elma wetted her hankie with some of Vernon's extra radiator water and rubbed the stain out.

Betty took the window and stuck her face through the vent. Mabel put her feet against the front seat and made churches and people with her hands, and the old lady was wrapped around herself again, her legs in a spiral beneath her dress.

Elma stretched in her seat, her arms behind her head. "We must be getting there."

"Must be," Vernon answered.

They passed through miles of kudzu, and the air was full of honeysuckle. The fields had been plowed and planted, and in the center of many were fenced-off family plots, the stones in short, angled rows. In the middle of one row, a large live oak had been burnt and split by lightning, and its heart was black as an upright vein of coal.

Then they were past the fields, and the ground changed to red cracked clay that sloped up and away from the road and became small hills. Ahead, the sky was empty, and on either side the pines came together in dark, raggedy lines. A large sign directed them off to the right and down a bumpy dirt road through the cool pine woods.

The entrance to the hospital appeared suddenly, a brick arch held up by two low walls that ran a few yards to either side and stopped. "GET WELL" was spelled across the arch in large, white wooden letters. The hospital was brick, too, an old building, three stories high in the middle and two stories on each wing. On either side of the drive were azaleas long past bloom, covered with rusty, drooping leaves.

Vernon parked in front of the main entrance. "You may get the surprise," he told Elma. "They may not be here for you to surprise them."

"And where do you think they could go?" She turned to the

girls. "Now, if they kiss you, hold your breath. I don't believe TB is ever cured for good, no matter what they say. And don't stare. You look like fools when you stare." She leaned over into the back seat. "Mother, we're here. Stop faking sleep. Open your eyes and fix yourself nice. Be nice, for Daddy's memory, if nothing else. He would want you to."

"I don't believe you can tell me what he might want. And right this minute I can feel some wild creature coming after my sow."

"Nonsense. Don't think you are going to stay in this car all day. We come a long way." Elma looked into the rearview mirror and drew her lipstick around her mouth in a tight, red bow, then put her hankie over her lips and blotted them.

Vernon came back and sat on the curb. The twins would come to meet them. Elma leaned her seat forward. "Out, Girls! They're coming." She walked around to the other side of the car. "Come on, you too."

Vernon lay on his back in the grass. "Vernon, do something with your mother!" She yelled a second time, and he came around to her. He leaned forward, but the heat of the car roof made him jerk upright. He stuck his hands in his pockets.

"If they want to see me, let 'em come see me," the old lady said. Her eyes were open, but she stared at a point past Vernon and Elma.

Elma stepped back, into Mabel. "See, you're already underfoot, acting like fools. Shut them mouths." She spit on her hankie and wiped a spot of dirt from Betty's forehead. Her braids were loose, and Elma pushed them behind the small pitcher ears. She pulled the skirt of Mabel's dress down and ran her hand over each sweat-dampened forehead, then leaned into the car to check herself in the mirror.

Past the mirror and across the lawn, a group of people were gathered under a large loblolly pine. There was a nurse in white and several men in blue striped bathrobes, and under the tree was a person in a wicker wheelchair. She squinted and saw that it was a man with only one leg. The nurse led one of the men away, and the man in the wheelchair turned his back to Elma.

Mabel and Betty stood ready, holding hands by the side of the car. A man and a woman walked across the parking lot, the man in faded jeans and a denim work shirt, his hands behind him. The woman's dress was covered with bright pink flowers, and she wore work boots, half laced, and flesh-colored cotton stockings rolled down below her knees. They walked side by side and were the same height. Their hair was the silver and dull brown color of pine pitch, and the woman's was pulled into a loose knot at the top of her head. The man brushed the hair from his forehead with a broad, tanned hand. They stopped in front of the car, and their eyes were large, brown cow's eyes, like Vernon's.

Elma stared and felt sick, felt the heat come down on her like a heavy quilt. She knew the couple was staring back.

"Well, Vernon," the man said. Now the woman put her hands behind her back, and Elma saw that the man and woman had the same face, the exact same face, and she looked from one to the other, seeing the man's face on the woman's body, then the woman's face on his. She put her knuckles in Mabel's back and pushed her. "This here is your niece, Mabel. Say hello, Mabel." Then Elma pulled Betty to her, so that she stood even with Mabel, directly in front of the twins. The girls looked up at the couple, then down at the ground.

Vernon sat up and lit a cigarette. "Sister," he pointed to the man, "this here's my wife, Elma. Sarie." Sarie, the woman, nodded at Elma.

Elma stared hard, shaded her eyes and saw the flesh of Sister's breasts underneath the shirt. They sagged in the same shape as Sarie's. They were the same long, flat breasts. Sister squatted and smiled at the girls. She was missing many teeth.

"We come a long way for this," Elma said. She did not know how she was able to say a word in the heat. "It's nice to meet you, real nice." Sister had a hand on Mabel's shoulder. Sarie nodded and smiled at Elma.

Elma saw the old lady in the back seat, her lips moving but no sound coming out, and Elma knew that she was laughing, at the whole thing, and at her. In a hard whisper, Elma said, "Vernon, get up! What are you doing?"

Family Visit

He sat up and looked at her, then lay down, one arm behind his head. "What the hell does it look like I am doing?"

"Well, we come here for a nice family visit, and now nobody seems to want to." She turned around to face the twins again. "Tired right out. Must be the heat. We should have us some tea, and we'll all feel better. I got some left from dinner."

"No, thank you," Sister said, and Elma heard the voice for the first time, a woman's voice, not what it should be, but nothing was what it should be.

"You know, my girls never seen identical twins till you. You're the only ones. They talk about it all the time, don't you, girls?"

Mabel looked up at her mother. "Yes, ma'am." Betty nodded, her thumb in her mouth.

"Betty don't suck her thumb all the time, just when she's tired," Elma said. She reached behind and grabbed Vernon's knee, turned around to face him. He pointed up at the sky. A large hawk crossed beneath the sun and passed over the woods behind the hospital. "Wish I brought my gun."

"Good God, Vernon, we come her to visit, not to shoot at the sky." Her mouth was dry, and she felt her lips crack. "We should have some fun, tell stories, get familiar. Do something, Vernon! Dear God!" She couldn't catch her breath, and, when she did, she felt sick and held her hands to her heart.

Betty sat down on the curb, and Mabel talked about the rabbits as she tried to pull Betty back to her feet. Sister smiled at the girls. "What other animals do you have?"

"Don't they look like their daddy, though?" Elma had to do something, anything, to keep from being sick.

"The pig, it's my granny's, but my daddy slops it." Mabel grasped for the center of attention. "My mama dresses us alike sometimes. I love to be twins." Betty pulled free of Mabel and got into the car. She lay down on the seat, close to her grandmother.

Elma knelt in the grass in front of Vernon. He got up and walked past her, and she was left with her back to the twins. She covered her face with her hands and wept until she could stop, then sat back on her heels and took a deep breath. "Why can't anything ever be nice?" she whispered.

Vernon pulled her to her feet, and she put her face on his chest, in the tart, familiar smells of him, sweat and tobacco, and the smell of her own kitchen.

"Glad to see you looking so fit," he said to the twins. Elma heard the words roll around in his chest. "The heat's got to Elma." He rubbed her back.

"Bye, y'all," Sister said. "We got to go in now. Sunday supper." She took Sarie's hand, and they walked back across the parking lot. Elma turned to watch, their exact strides, their flat and identical backs.

"That's that," Vernon said. He guided Elma into the front seat and closed the door after her and Mabel. Betty sat in her grandmother's lap and twisted a piece of the old lady's hair around and around her finger.

"Why is Mama crying?" Mabel asked.

"The heat, baby," Vernon said. Tears and sweat ran down Elma's face. She wiped it dry on the bottom of her blouse. Vernon honked the horn, and the twins turned and waved. There was a crack of thunder, and they ran in funny, crooked steps to the door of the hospital.

"Vernon, you got some explaining to do. And don't think I'm going to be making up to your family no more. You better be telling me why you let this happen."

"Curiosity killed the cat."

"Huh? Oh. Well, I ain't satisfied. We need us some fun somehow." She blew her nose on the dirty hankie and pushed her hair behind her ears. "We can still stop for our treat, ice cream."

The girls yelled, and Mabel clapped her hands. Vernon looked into the rearview mirror at her, and she stopped.

"That's something, girls, the way they look alike, even when they try not to? They probably dress like that so they can be told apart. Ain't that so, Vernon?"

"Must be."

"You girls missed the man with only one leg. He was in a wheelchair. I should have hollered for you. Next time. I know another sight, though. I'll show you where me and your daddy was married, the very courthouse. Your granny missed out on that, too."

"The rain'll break this heat spell anyway," Vernon said. "I believe we're going to get caught right in the middle of it."

Testimony

Eddie Cantwell had a mission, and it was the only thing in his mind, the only thing in front of him. It was the fourth day after Rebecca's death, and he and his son, Martin, had walked for three of those days. A mockingbird called, and the river moved muddy and slow below them. Eddie picked a dogwood flower, the same flat white of his linen suit, and put it in his buttonhole, then pulled himself up the bank to the edge of the road and waited for Martin. "Another day, son, another day from the Lord," he called down.

Martin was two heads taller than his father and a mute. He wore bib overalls, and, in one hand, he carried their belongings in a faded, blue flour sack: straight razor, small white enamel pot, two tin mugs, writing tablet, large lead pencil, pair of brown wool socks, and a wooden cigar box. In his other hand, he carried a pair of men's black hightop shoes. Like Eddie, he was barefoot. He stepped back, then climbed the bank at a run.

* * *

When Rebecca took sick, Eddie had put her in a private hospital, in a clean, light ward, her bed by a window that looked out on a magnolia. He had taken good care of her, had not fulfilled the prophecy her daddy had made: "Run off with a stranger, girl, and you'll be sure to fall." There was, in the end, nothing Eddie could do. Day by day, she weakened, and her skin turned dry and thin as a spiderweb. When the cost of the room became more than Eddie could bear, she was moved to the county hospital and the wretched ward where she died. It was a bunch, the doctor told Eddie, a bunch inside that killed her.

*   *   *

Eddie and Martin walked at a constant pace, beyond the riverbed and then through fresh fields. It was midmorning before they came to a crossroad. Ahead was dirt, and to the right and left was dirt, the poor, brown color of an eggshell. Eddie turned to Martin. "What would your mother say, boy?"

Martin shrugged and shifted the flour sack to his other hand.

"I believe she would want our comfort," Eddie said. He headed to the right, where he could see shade further down the road.

They walked in a narrow valley under a canopy of huge oaks. Martin trudged, never even stopped to wipe the sweat from his face, and Eddie walked double-time to keep up with him.

He was about worn out when they came to a house. Two molting hens pecked around the base of a chinquapin, and an old baldheaded man sat in a rocker on the porch. He spit into a small washtub at his feet and stared at Eddie. Eddie stood directly in front of the man and bowed his head. "Sir, we need water," he said. "We got our own cups." He stepped closer to the porch.

"Around back." The old man wore a union suit and beneath the moth holes his skin was pale and brittle. He held a threadbare quilt in his curled fingers.

Martin hauled up the bucket. There was a nickel-sized hole near the bottom, and Eddie held their cups under it. Then, in turn, they raised the bucket over one another and let the cold water run down their backs. They they walked side by side around the other end of the house, past a bed of scrawny red hollyhocks at the corner. Beneath the fuzzy, yellow stalks lay a small, black dog. He followed them and growled at their backs.

"He's no harm," the old man called.

At the sound of the voice, the dog ran past Eddie and Martin, but his short legs could not carry him up the single step. He cried and wagged his thin tail. Eddie picked him up and set him on the porch.

"I ask for your kindness," Eddie said. "My late wife was a Hodge, Rebecca Grace. Do you know of her people?" Eddie held his hands in front of him, open as if he carried something small. He stared at them, at the ridges of callous across the fingers and palms.

The old man wedged the little dog between his knees and looked past Eddie at Martin. He took after his mother, with small ears, milk-blue eyes, and a good chin. "Know of them," the old man said.

"I have a mission, me and this boy, her boy, do. To find them people and put her in their care." The sun reached the peak of the house, and Eddie covered his eyes and stepped forward into the shade.

"Won't be finding them." The man leaned across the dog and spit. "Them Hodges left this part."

Eddie turned around and sat on the step. A rooster strutted and lifted his bright green and black wings. The hens had found dust holes under the chinquapin. The rooster scratched and crowed before he disappeared around the corner beneath the hollyhocks.

"Picked up and left," the old man said.

"Martin, give me that testimony." Eddie spoke as if he hadn't heard. He was not sure that he had or whether what the old man said was important.

Martin reached into the sack and brought out the tablet. On the cover was an Indian in a red and black feather bonnet. Eddie looked at each page, then stopped and read: "Please lay me to rest on the Hodge land in Ewall County."

"The land is still there," the old man said.

"That ain't the whole of it: And let them hear the testimony of my faith."

The dog jumped from the old man's lap and barked. Eddie turned to see a wrinkled, bare foot, the yellow color of the rooster's scaly legs, reach from under the quilt and prod the dog.

"Hush, Sam," the old man said. "That's a piece of business

you got."

"That it is, sir, a real piece of business."

"Well, I can't be the one to help." From his chest came the sound of knuckles on a washboard, and he leaned close to the bucket, but nothing came out of him.

A young woman pushed the screen door open. She had shoulders so narrow she appeared to have no neck, and her tallow-colored hair was coiled in a braid on top of her head. "I have got dinner," she said. She held the screen and nodded to Eddie and Martin. The old man stood and pulled the quilt up over his bent back. "There'll be plenty."

They ate at a table that was a shed door set on four small hickory logs. The woman served them cornbread, greens, and salt pork gravy. Then she leaned against the cold stove, arms across her breasts, and watched.

The old man smacked his bare gums, and, with his curved fingers, he pushed the food into his mouth. Somewhere at the back of the house a baby cried, and dark spots of milk soaked the bodice of the woman's dress. She left the kitchen and came back with a fat, naked boy on her hip. He grabbed at her dress and pulled her breast free. "I heard what you was saying," the woman said. "I knew them people."

Martin held his empty plate up to her, and she served him with her free hand. The baby let go of her breast with a loud sucking noise and waved at Eddie. Pale milk ran down the corners of its mouth.

"I remember when they left," she said. "It was the year my brother Willy was born. The bloody flux took babies. Willy, lots of cousins. Then there was tainted water. Them that drank it, their throats closed up on them. Right up."

Eddie crumbled corn bread into his buttermilk. Flies were clustered in the corners of the small, dirty windowpanes. "When was that?"

The woman sat down and held the baby across her lap. "A good eight years now," she said.

Eddie walked to the door and put his hands in his pockets. Through the layers of worn cloth, he felt his skin.

"The land's still there," the old man said. He wiped his

mouth and chin with the quilt.

*   *   *

Grass grew in the middle of the road through Hodge Hollow, and the dogwood was still in bloom along both steep sides. In the late afternoon, there were no bird songs, and the empty air was damp and cool.

The Hodge place stood end to end on the ridge. Two windows had looked out across the mountains, and between them was a lilac, its branches long and thin and bare. There were no doors, and Eddie looked straight through, from one end of the house to the other. He stepped onto the underflooring. Between the kitchen and the middle was the arch Rebecca had spoken of, a curve of soft, old wood. Eddie turned around and took in the whole of the house, three rooms and a sleeping loft. He felt himself inside a skeleton. "She had a lot of love for such a meager place."

He and Martin watched the sky dim at sunset. They made their beds in a shed that smelled of sugar cure and smoke. Martin slept stretched out on his belly, his hand on the sack. Eddie folded his trousers for a pillow and spread his jacket across his legs. He listened for the only sounds Martin had ever made, the small noises of sleep.

In the morning, the mountains were gray-blue in the early sun. They walked a short way along the ridge, traced the limits of the fields to the orchard, and beyond, the family plot, a row of wooden markers in a small clearing covered with wild strawberries. Two graves had sunk below ground level, one the size of a baby.

A bramble-choked path led to the spring. Eddie shaved with cold water and no soap, but he could not feel anything, not even the scrape of the dull razor across his cheek. Martin's beard was new, no more than black wisps in a few spots.

They turned back, down the same paths and tracks, past an empty cabin where a sow came from inside followed by nine piglets, past a large, black mass of cinder and ash where a place had burned, through the Hodge land and out again. When they got to the tar road, Martin stayed on the dirt shoulder.

Testimony

There was one small house, then another, with flower beds under the windows, red and orange zinnias, more hollyhocks, faded irises. The houses were set close together, and in front were shade trees, oak and elm. A truck passed through the intersection. Eddie and Martin stood at the beginning of the sidewalk. "Dear Lord, see us through," Eddie said.

The town of Ewall sat in a giant thumbprint in the valley. The mountains sloped to its center, to the park and the fountain in the shape of a mountain woman, the water spewing from her bucket, to the courthouse and wooden belltower, to the Only Salvation Baptist Church. A single paved road passed through Ewall and on to the next county.

Eddie and Martin sat on the cement edge of the fountain and watched two little girls climb over the rim and sit down. The water was up to their waists. A woman called out, and they jumped up and ran around the inside of the fountain and laughed as they climbed back over the edge. "You were the true joy of your mother's life," Eddie said. He and Martin waved at the little girls, and the mother waved back.

Eddie left Martin at the fountain and went across to the courthouse. His bare footsteps echoed with a slap against the stone floor. The hall was two stories high, and directly below the dome was a woman at a desk.

She had a hair net over her short, curly brown hair. She smiled and dropped her eyeglasses down to the end of her nose.

"I have a testimony to give," Eddie said. "It's my wife's, Rebecca Grace Hodge. Her testimony of faith."

"You're free to preach, Mr. Hodge. You don't need a permit."

He backed away. "I'm Cantwell, Eddie Cantwell," he said. "Thank you."

*   *   *

Martin stood at the edge of the fountain. The little girls had come back, joined by two boys, older and bigger, who floated small, silver boats made from tinfoil. The girls stood at a distance, and one of them wrung the water out of her skirt, twisting the fabric in her hands. Eddie watched until Martin saw him, then together they went around the fountain and out the other end of town.

The houses were only on one side of the road, across from a steep bank. In front of one, a woman in a big, black bonnet sat on an upturned bucket and worked a butter churn. Eddie stopped twice to wipe the sweat from his eyes before the road took a sharp swing around a red clay bank.

In the cleft of the crossroads was a freshly whitewashed store and, in front of it, an ox cart, a single dun-colored ox in the yoke. Behind the store, an unplowed field went back as far as Eddie could see. Two men sat in straight-backed chairs on the porch. They followed Eddie and Martin inside.

Martin stood behind Eddie, so close that Eddie could feel Martin breathe, his chest filling and pressing against Eddie's back. There was the smell of turpentine and pickle brine, the creak of the unoiled fan overhead, and the sound of hundreds of flies caught on paper. Eddie made out the storekeeper in back of the counter, and the two men from the porch leaned against a wall of canned goods. A third man sat on a milking stool.

"Sardines, please, and crackers and Coca-Cola," Eddie said.

The storekeeper used a hook to pull a flat can from a high shelf, then filled a small brown bag with crackers. "Soda's right back of you. You boys coming or going?"

"Some of both." Eddie counted out two dimes and four nickels onto the counter. "I got me a piece of business. I got to follow the wishes of the dead. My wife passed five days now, and she directed me to return her and her words to her people. She was a Hodge, Rebecca Grace."

"Hodge. Hodge Hollow," the storekeeper said. He wore an apron advertising baking powder.

"I got to bury her and give her testimony of faith."

One of the men spoke. "That's a trial."

"That it is. I got no out. I'm going to give her testimony to any that will listen, and then I got to take a burial collection. Now, please. Me and my boy is about to perish." He held the bag and cans up to them. "This business is beating us."

There was no breeze, and the white sides of the building

were brilliant in the sun, but the air was less close than inside. Martin opened the soda bottles on the edge of the roof, then he and Eddie sat in the shade of the overhang.

From inside, the storekeeper said, "You boys feeling some better?" Eddie stood as the man came onto the porch.

"Why, yes we do, thank you, sir. I forgot my manners. This here's my boy, Martin, and I'm Eddie Cantwell."

Martin put his hand out and stepped forward, onto the crackers. He saw what he had done and moved back against the wall.

"Pleased. I'm Rawlins, Judd Rawlins." The storekeeper nodded and smiled. He had gold caps on his front teeth. "I know what a trial is. I've had mine."

"I am short on time as well as money, Mr. Rawlins. I got to get my wife from the funeral parlor before another four days, or there's nothing to be done. She'll go to public lots. I got to have thirty-four dollars."

"The only thing is to get that money, and get your wife, and get her back here. That's the answer."

Mr. Rawlins took brown paper and wrote with a piece of coal, "Testimony of Rebecca Grace Hodge. In Ewall. Given by her beloved family." He hung it on the new white wall, and Eddie went across the road to see if it was plain enough.

"Don't study your troubles too long," Mr. Rawlins cautioned. He offered Eddie and Martin a bed in his home. "No, sir," Eddie said. "We sleep better under the stars. If it don't rain."

When they got back to town, the sky was overcast. Eddie felt his legs move and his mouth open, like a mechanical bank stuck in motion. He lay under a sycamore while Martin sat on the rim of the fountain with his feet in the water.

Eddie awoke from a dream in which he stood at the edge of a sheer cliff of shiny black coal. He yelled but there was no echo. His mouth formed words, and, over and over, he yelled. The words were important, perhaps the most important sounds he had ever made. When he was fully awake, he tried to remember what he had said. He was certain that the dream was timely and that he would keep it in his mind for a long while. Next to him, Martin slept. Someone had put a cover

over him.

In the morning of the sixth day, Eddie and Martin had corn-bread and Coca-Cola brought to them by Mr. Rawlins's wife, a round woman with a thin smile. She took their hands in hers and prayed. "I am privileged to help in a matter of faith," she said.

Eddie lettered a notice on tablet paper with the same words Mr. Rawlins had used. "Stop at each place and hold it out," he told Martin. "Follow the sun, and when it's noon, turn around and come back. I'll be right here." He took the shoes and sack and pushed Martin in the right direction.

Eddie spent the morning under the sycamore. He leaned his ear against the tree every so often, imagined that he heard something, maybe even the sap running, but he knew that all he heard was his own blood in his ears. It was trading day, and he was an attraction in town, greeted by people who had heard of his mission. Each time someone came to him, he stood and felt humble.

When Martin returned, the grass around the fountain was covered with red and yellow oilcloths, worn quilts, and stitched-together sacks. Women set out dinner and pulled small children from the edge of the fountain. Wagons were hitched in front of the courthouse, and there were automobiles and pickups parked along the street. Mr. Rawlins came for Eddie and led him and Martin around the corner to a mule wagon with a long wooden bed. "It's for your use," he said. Eddie pulled Martin to him, hugged his waist. "It's her chariot, son."

The young woman who had told Eddie of the Hodge bad luck brought fried chicken wrapped in waxed paper for Martin and Eddie, but Eddie had no taste for it. Part of his grief let go and he sobbed, unable to stop until he took a deep breath, but the smells of food and people and tobacco smoke made him heave. He dipped his hands in the tepid water and splashed his face.

Eddie lifted his head, and the crowd quieted. He read from the tablet in a flat high-pitched voice: "Dear Mother and Daddy. I know these are my last words to you. I am sending Martin and Eddie to you because, even if you have not forgiven me,

Testimony

I know that the Lord has. I want to go back to the place I love on this earth, lay my body to rest when my soul is at peace." Eddie took a deep breath. "I can smell the flowers," he went on. "Roses on the churchyard fence. Lilac outside the window. And sweet william and violets. I can see the garden now, Eddie. And our little lost baby is here, too. I will miss you so, but I will be here when you get here."

Eddie dropped the tablet to the ground. "I was in that room, and I can tell you there was not a sweet smell in it. There was seven in it with her, and it had the smell of death, of proud flesh. And the whole while she was seeing and smelling the flowers of the heavenly garden."

He was finished, dry-eyed and dry-throated. Next to him, Martin's big body shuddered as he cried. Eddie pulled the cigar box out and arranged its contents. He draped the yellowed lace, Rebecca's last piece, on the lid of the box, and, next to it, he set out three small, sepia photographs. In the middle was Rebecca, round-faced and serious. Her hair fell to her waist, dark and fine. Her mother's wedding picture showed a fair and pretty young woman holding an open Bible. In his photograph, Mr. Hodge held baby Rebecca on his lap, her features small copies of his, but her eyes were wide, almost in fright. Eddie motioned for people to come to him, and they stopped at the box, then went to where Mr. Rawlins stood under the sycamore with a tin can in his hand.

Mr. Rawlins traded the silver for paper money, and Eddie carried forty-three dollars in the pocket of his jacket. "I do not want to take the nine dollars over, but I can't take no chance," he told the storekeeper.

*   *   *

The undertaker had thick, white sideburns and wore overalls like Martin's over a starched, white shirtfront. A stiff, black bow tie circled his neck where his collar should have been. He led Eddie and Martin down a wallpapered hall, past a room where polished pine coffins were stacked in piles of three. They walked through the kitchen and the smell of sausage and out into the backyard. There was a clothesline hung with muslin sheets and, at the far end of the yard, a rough lumber shed.

Inside the shed, Rebecca's coffin sat on saw horses between two blocks of ice. The undertaker held the door open for them, and Martin took the lead while Eddie guided the box between the sawhorses and kicked them out of his way.

When they had the coffin in the cart, Eddie counted out thirty-four dollars and two more. The undertaker took it and tipped an imaginary hat.

*   *   *

At Mr. Rawlins's store, Eddie bought two brass handles, a brass plate that read "At Rest," and cross-shaped coffin screws. The man on the milking stool was there, and he lifted his hand to Eddie and called him preacher. He kept his head down and whittled at a piece of pine. "I'll have the cart and mule back before dark," Eddie told Mr. Rawlins.

Martin tried to use the edge of the plate to screw on a handle, but the plate was too wide, so Eddie went back into the store to borrow a screwdriver and a shovel. The man on the stool looked up, and Eddie saw that he was blind. He grabbed the bottom of Eddie's jacket.

"In your hand you got pretty much all I got left in the world," Eddie said.

The blind man stood and felt his way up to Eddie's face. His hands moved around Eddie's head with the dry flutter of bat wings. "You're young," the man said. "You got time."

*   *   *

Eddie and Martin left the wagon at the beginning of the rise to the Hodge place and carried the casket between them. Martin held the shovel and sack in one hand. His grip slipped and the casket pitched. The sound it gave was slight, and Eddie wondered if Rebecca was indeed inside. The sound was like pine branches in a small gust of wind.

The apple blossoms had gone by, and a swarm of bees passed above the trees, a wide, black cloud of noise and the smell of honey. Eddie thought of his dream and saw a swarm of bees come out of his mouth, and then an echo across the valley, back and forth until it was a whisper.

Martin sat at the head of the grave and watched Eddie dig, then took his turn with the shovel. The hole needed be only as deep as Eddie's waist, and, when it was dug, they got on their knees to let the casket down and kept hold of the handles until it was settled at the bottom. While Eddie said the prayer and verses he knew, they moved side by side around the edges of the grave and with their feet pushed the rich dirt onto the casket. He said the Hundredth Psalm and the Twenty-third, the Beatitudes, the Ten Commandments, and the Lord's Prayer, again and again. When he felt no more dirt and opened his eyes, it was almost sundown. He smoothed the mound and tamped it down as best he could, then sent Martin to return the shovel and the mule and wagon.

Clouds drifted across the rising moon. Eddie gathered wood and laid a fire, then squatted and struck a match with his thumbnail. The twigs caught, and he blew on the sparks at the base of the fire. Apple wood gave the smoke a sweet smell.

Sweat ran down his sides and the back of his neck. He undressed, removing his jacket, then his trousers. His wedding suit was done for, hardly more than pieces of old linen, and his shirt was like cheesecloth. He shed it, too, and laid the clothes on the ground, then moved back from the fire. From the sack he took the cigar box and the tablet. One by one, he tore the pages from the tablet and held each over the flames. The heat lifted them, floated them above the fire, before they fell. Then he held the photographs in a small fan and pulled them out, one by one. At the edge of the fire, the cigar box began to burn. The clouds uncovered a wide patch of stars and the moon, and in that light Eddie turned and made his way to the Hodge place.

He stood naked. He could make out the tops of the apple trees and thought he could see beneath them to the light of his fire. He was holding the lace in a fist so tight he had to pry it open with his other hand. Then, in the doorway of the abandoned house, he balanced on the sill with one foot in front of the other and held on with both hands. He pulled his small, spent body toward the door jamb, the wood cool against his forehead, and he held it for a moment, then pulled back and brought his forehead against the wood again, over and over, until he smelled blood and felt it wet on his face, but no pain, and he did not stop until hard fists hit his bony body, until Martin pulled him to the ground.